Resurrection of Evil!

Then the lights went out. She was helpless in the dank, cavernous wine cellar. Then suddenly from a distance she heard a low, gloating chuckle—a malevolent sound that sent her fears soaring!

Wheeling around she snapped her flashlight beam in the direction of the sound. To her utter shock, she saw the outline of a crouching figure in some sort of ragged robe. Then the beam leveled on the features of a gargoyle with a twisted mouth and glittering, insane eyes.

Vanessa screamed and stumbled into total blackness. . . .

THE BRIDES
OF SATURN

Marilyn Ross

A BERKLEY MEDALLION BOOK
published by
BERKLEY PUBLISHING CORPORATION

THE BRIDES OF SATURN

Chapter One

The Brides of Saturn!

Vanessa Masters felt that the strangest thing about it all was that before her marriage she had only the most casual interest in astrology. Yet suddenly it was to become the great influence in her life! Or to be more exact, it was to be the frightening avenue to her rendezvous with death! That she had been born a Capricorn soon became of the utmost consequence to her, since it was because she was a daughter of January that she had come under the death curse!

From her childhood she'd always had a powerful fear of death. Perhaps this was because her mother, while still a lovely young woman, had become ill and died within a few months. Vanessa had never fully recovered from the pain and shock of the death of her actress mother. She had watched her on the stage and thought of her as someone eternally beautiful. At the age of seven it had seemed to her that her parents were immortal, and then this shadow of death had enveloped her gentle mother.

Her actor father had borne the tragedy well and given Vanessa, an only child, all the love and interest of which he was capable. But his career often took him away from her. She grew up in a small town in Sussex, where a cousin of her mother lived. She became one of a family of four children, and in its way it was a wholesome manner of life

1

for her. But she never got over missing her mother, and she never was as happy as when her actor father, James Masters, came to Sussex from a season in the West End, or months on tour of the provinces, to visit her.

These were the magic times of her growing up. She loved to hear her father talk of his theatrical experiences and have him quote to her from the roles in the many famous plays in which he'd acted. Yet, from the start, she'd guessed that he was carefully keeping her away from a theatrical atmosphere. He wanted her to grow up in wholesome small-town surroundings without direct contact with the stage.

But she knew the theater was in her veins. At every opportunity she and one of her female cousins went to the town cinema to see the latest films. And at the rare intervals when a touring theater company visited the town, she always managed to attend. Watching the live actors on the stage was an almost mystical experience for her.

And despite some minor objections from her father, she acted in every school play. And when the school drama instructor told her she had real talent, it was the happiest moment in all her young life. It was about that time she began to read the plays of Shakespeare until she could quote passages from many of them. And in *Measure for Measure* she found the Bard of Avon expressing the dark fears which she, herself, felt about death. A chill ran down her spine as she read: "The weariest and most loathed worldly life, That age, ache, penury and imprisonment, Can lay on nature, is a paradise, to what we fear of death."

Vanessa found herself regarded by her school companions as serious and determined. She was spoken of as old for her age by her elders, and looked upon as a very plain child whose black, stringy hair was in unflattering contrast

2

to her milk-white skin. Yet a second look could have told anyone that her fine, even features had potential. And her slender, lithe body would surely fill out and be pleasantly graceful.

Vanessa experienced most of these miracles of change by the time she was seventeen. The exciting climax to her year of graduation from the town school was her playing the role of Nora in the school's production of Ibsen's *A Doll's House.* It was the most important role she'd ever had, and it came at precisely the right moment. She had developed into a lovely young girl with bewitching almond-green eyes, black hair in a straight flattering cut with bangs, plus a generous mouth that could quickly offer the most beguiling of smiles. The local audience fell in love with her.

James Masters happened to be between roles and so was able to attend the closing performance of the show. After the curtain came down, the headmistress and other teachers on the staff served tea and cakes for the students participating in the play and their parents. Vanessa sat with her father, feeling very conspicuous.

She knew that many eyes were upon them, since her distinguished-looking gray-haired father was known to be an actor. Her pride in him was only diminished by her wish that this could be a more private celebration for them—and by the cool enthusiasm with which her father had received her playing of Nora.

The buxom headmistress came to them with some extra cakes and smiled knowingly at James Masters. "I must say, Vanessa has inherited your talent, Mr. Masters. Wasn't she lovely in the play?"

"Very interesting," her father observed primly as he took a piece of cake. "But then, her mother was also a

3

very successful actress until her death.''

''Really?'' the headmistress said sympathetically. ''How sad that she died so young.''

''Yes, it was,'' Vanessa's father agreed quietly.

The mention of her mother's death brought a moment of shadow to Vanessa. And as the schoolmistress moved on, she asked her father, ''Did I remind you of mother on the stage?''

The distinguished face was suddenly sad. ''Yes,'' he said. ''You resemble her a great deal. Even in your acting. And of course, you're the same type. She was also born a Capricorn, you know.''

''Was my mother interested in astrology? Did my being born under the same sign as she was mean something to her?''

''It interested her,'' James Masters said. ''She was much more into astrology than I have ever been.''

''I know hardly anything about it,'' Vanessa mused. And then she asked, ''Did you honestly think I was good in the play?''

''Yes.'' Then her father added, ''For an amateur.''

''Thank you,'' she said gratefully. ''I love the theater and acting. I want to make it my life. I want to attend theater college.''

Her handsome father looked shocked. ''You can't mean that! Being an actor is a gypsy's life. I don't want it for you!''

''Why not? You are in the theater, and so was Mother.''

Her father raised a protesting hand. ''And being in the theater, I know the dark side of it. It's not all glamour and big salaries. Mostly it's struggle and eking out a bare existence. I've been lucky, and I'm still only a minor actor at Stratford!''

4

"I'm proud of you!" Vanessa said sincerely.

"Whether you're proud of me or not, we must face the facts," her father said. "And the facts are that I'm not a financial success. It's only due to a small legacy from my family that I've managed to give you what I have and still remain in the theater. And when I die, you'll have a scant bequest from me."

"Don't talk of dying!" she protested.

"These things must be considered," her father said. "I don't want you at the mercy of the West End wolves. I want you to have an education. A degree that will enable you to earn your living no matter what happens."

She was stubborn, as was her custom. She said, "I want to go on the stage! It's the only thing I care about!"

Her father looked unhappy. "You know how much you mean to me. I find it hard to deny you any wish. But I want better things for you."

"I care only for the theater!"

He stared at her, and then, after a moment of hesitation, he said, "Let me suggest something."

"I want to go to London and look for an acting job!"

James Masters said, "You need a great deal more training before you attempt that. You were fine in this school play, but the professional theater is another thing, with much higher standards."

"Don't you think I can meet them with training?"

"Possibly with training," he said. "I'll tell you what. Why can't we compromise?"

She was disappointed and hurt at his wish to keep her off the stage. "How can we compromise in a thing like this?"

"Let me explain," her father said. "Before I was offered my present post with the Stratford-on-Avon Com-

5

pany, I went without work for many months.''

''You didn't tell me,'' Vanessa said, her green almond eyes concerned.

''There are many things about my theater career of which I haven't spoken,'' her father said gravely. ''In any event, I was worried and without prospect of work. A friend of mine who is associated with the Drama Center London told me of an opening on their staff for an instructor. I went and saw the principal and was much impressed with the school. I almost took the job, but the opportunity to go to Stratford came along.''

''So?''

''So I know a good deal about this school and its methods. I'd like you to take their three-year course.''

Her fine-featured, intelligent face at once glowed. ''But that is exactly what I want!''

''Wait!'' her father said. ''I want you to take their teachers' training course in speech and drama rather than their professional acting course. This will give you a degree to teach in any school or college, and at the same time you'll be working in the theater.''

Her spirits sank. ''That is not the same as being on the stage.''

''I'd call it better. There is always work for teachers!''

''But I want to be an actress, not a teacher!'' she complained.

''Take this training,'' her father said. ''Then, if you still want to be on the stage professionally, you can try it. You'll have the added basic training you need, and you'll be twenty when you finish. That's young enough to attack the West End.''

So it was settled. The compromise was made. But Vanessa was not the sort to have her ambitions put aside easily. All during her student days at the Drama Center London she made use of every opportunity to study the professional acting course as well. Her diligence impressed her instructors, and they encouraged her in this.

Margaret Vincent, one of the senior dramatic coaches, directed a production of Somerset Maugham's *The Constant Wife* and assigned Vanessa to the leading role. Once again she scored and won the approval of all the school's staff.

The thin, ascetic Margaret Vincent told her afterward, "I can't understand why you're seeking a degree in teaching. You are a born actress."

Vanessa smiled. "I feel I am. But my father doesn't want me on the stage."

"Yet he is an actor!" her instructor said.

"It's the way he feels. So I'm doing as he asked. Getting my teacher's degree, and then I'm heading straight for the theater agencies and the casting calls. I have no plans to teach. I'm going on the stage professionally."

Her teacher shook her head. "You're a strange girl, Vanessa. But I think you'll succeed. Once you make your mind up about something, you really work for it."

It was true. And the day that Vanessa received her degree in dramatic coaching, she told her father, "I've done all you asked. Now I'm going to try the West End."

James Masters kissed her and smiled ruefully. "I might have known. All right. Have a go at it. I wish you luck. And don't think it will be easy."

So Vanessa began her assault on London. And as her father had predicted, it wasn't easy. She had several offers to take stock acting jobs in provincial cities and turned them down. It was either going to be London or nothing as far as she was concerned. Since no agent would take her on as a client and the casting calls were always over-crowded, it began to look as if she would become a teacher after all.

Then she ran into a friend from her student days in Piccadilly Circus one afternoon. The girl's name was Mary Brady and she'd been in the professional acting class at the school. She was a blond, attractive girl with an outgoing manner. Her mother was a wardrobe mistress and her father a stage manager, so she came by her acting ambitions honestly.

Standing on the busy sidewalk on this bleak October afternoon they exchanged greetings, and then the attractive Mary asked the inevitable question, "Are you working?"

"No!" Vanessa said mournfully. "I should give up, but I won't."

The trench-coated Mary said, "That doesn't sound like you."

"Sorry," she said with a bleak smile. "What about you?"

"I'm doing some bit parts in a revue at the Trocadero," Mary said. "It isn't the greatest, but everyone claims it will run at least a year."

"I wish you could find something in it for me," Vanessa said.

Mary's face lit up. "I've just thought of something. There is nothing in my show. But my mother is going to be wardrobe mistress for Augustus Gordon's new play. And they are having a casting call at the Aldwych in the morning. There are at least a couple of minor roles you could read."

Vanessa listened with interest. Augustus Gordon was

one of England's finest light-comedy players. He had starred in films and on Broadway as well as being a name in the West End. To be in an Augustus Gordon production in even a tiny part would be a wonderful way to begin her career.

She said, "Do you think I'd have any chance?"

Mary gave her a roguish wink. "I promise you will. Mother is a friend of the director, Ronny Walsh. I'll see that she mentions your name to him. When you show up for the audition, he'll at least have heard of you."

Vanessa was all excitement. "Can you really arrange that?"

"No trouble at all," Mary said. "You'll have to win a part on the basis of your own talent, but at least you'll get a hearing!"

Vanessa thanked her friend and went back to the tawdry boardinghouse near the theater district where she had a small back room. It was the first ray of hope in weeks. She had been on the point of writing her father and asking his help, but kept putting this off. Now she might finally get her chance.

But when she arrived at the Aldwych the next morning and saw the crowd of actors and actresses waiting to be auditioned, her heart sank. The alley outside the stage-door entrance was filled all the way to the street. She found herself near the end of the line, standing next to an enormously tall, thin man with a long, solemn face.

The tall man was dressed in shabby black, with a black homburg to match. He glanced at her and asked, "Have you ever worked with Augustus Gordon before?"

"No," she said dismally. "And by the look of this line, I'm not likely to ever work with him."

9

The tall man with the long, solemn face showed no expression at all as he said, "I wouldn't worry. Ronny Walsh is conducting the call. And he doesn't waste time getting through a crowd. He's very efficient. He's been directing Augustus Gordon's plays for years."

She stared up at the thin, tall man with new interest. "You sound as if you know him well."

"I do," the thin man agreed, with still no show of expression. "I specialize in butler's roles. I have been a butler in at least three of Augustus Gordon's starring vehicles. This present play is by Terence Rattigan, and there is an excellent butler's role. I have every expectation of getting it."

Vanessa was amused by his solemn mien and his unexpected optimism. She said, "I hope you do."

"What will you be reading for?" her companion in the line asked.

"One of the small parts. Really a walk-on," she said.

"Well, you're attractive enough," the solemn man said. "My name is Hobbs, Harrison Hobbs."

"I'm happy to meet you, Mr. Hobbs," she said. "My name is Vanessa Masters."

The tall man's eyebrows lifted. "You are not, by any chance, related to James Masters?"

She nodded proudly. "My father."

"Is that so?" Harrison Hobbs said, still showing no change of expression. "He is an excellent actor. Haven't seen him in years. Hear he's at Stratford."

"That's right," she volunteered.

Harrison Hobbs proved correct in his prediction that the line would melt more quickly than she'd expected. It seemed only a short while before they actually moved into the theater. Onstage a short, ruddy-faced man with pure white hair was conducting the auditions. She knew that he must be Ronny Walsh, the director. And seated at a table behind him was Augustus Gordon, with the air of someone supervising the entire affair. There was no mistaking his good-looking if slightly jaded countenance. He had twinkling black eyes under black arched brows, and his usual look was one of benign surprise.

Harrison Hobbs bowed to the seated Ronny Walsh and said, "I have been out of town, otherwise I expect you would have contacted me for the butler's role."

The pugnacious Ronny Walsh nodded. "Right, Hobbs. No need for you to read. You're hired."

"Thank you, sir," the tall character actor said, and went across the stage to discuss terms with the business manager of the project. The eminent Augustus Gordon deigned to give the tall man a patronizing smile as he passed by his table.

Ronny Walsh frowned slightly as Vanessa presented herself. He asked, "What's your name?"

"Vanessa Masters," she said in a nervous voice.

The ruddy-faced man showed recognition of her name. He said, "I have heard about you. You're James Masters' daughter, aren't you?"

"Yes," she replied, still nervous.

The director handed her a book of the play and instructed her, "Read the speech at the top of page forty-three."

She was so tense, the words blurred before her for a moment. Then she made her eyes focus properly, and she read the short, simple speech. She let the book drop from a reading level, and her eyes nervously fixed on the white-haired man.

Ronny Walsh turned to the thirtyish star of the comedy

and asked, "What do you think?"

Augustus Gordon nodded approval. "She's all right. We can use her."

The white-haired man turned to her again. "Fine," he said. "You're hired. Go and see about your contract."

Her heart pounding with excitement, she blurted out her thanks to the two. It seemed to her that the star was amused as she rushed by him to join the others who were being signed to contracts.

The business manager was brusque in manner. He named a sum that was smaller than she'd expected but on which she could manage. He asked, "You willing to sign for the run of the play and possible touring?"

"Yes," she said firmly. She knew she couldn't miss this, even though it was a small part.

"Very well," the business manager said, and hastily went about filling in her name and the terms on the contract. He then presented it to her with a bored air and told her, "Sign in the two places marked with an X."

She did, and automatically became a member of the company for the new Terence Rattigan play. She was standing there glowing with happiness when she became aware of someone new at her elbow. She glanced and saw that it was Augustus Gordon.

An amused twinkle showed in his lively black eyes again as he told her, "Jane put in a good word for you."

It took her a moment to realize he was talking about Mary Brady's mother, the wardrobe mistress of the company. She smiled and said, "That was good of her. I talked with her daughter yesterday. She's a friend of mine. We were in drama school together."

The star nodded. "This will be your first London show?"

"Yes," she agreed. She thought it better not to let him know that it would be her first professional appearance anywhere.

He said, "According to Jane, you are the daughter of James Masters."

"I am," she agreed, not entirely surprised that her father's name had come up again. It seemed the theater world consisted of a fairly small circle.

"I worked with him several times when I was starting in the business," Augustus Gordon said. "He's a fine actor. If you have inherited any of his talent, you should go far."

"Thank you," she said.

Then the famous star surprised her by saying, "I'm on my way to lunch. Would you care to join me, or have you some other plans?"

Startled by the unexpected invitation, she hesitated and then managed, "I haven't any other plans."

"Then come along," he said. "I have a table waiting for me at the Lamb and Flag."

Vanessa let him guide her offstage and out the stage door. He talked pleasantly about the play and his hopes that it would have a long run. She said hardly anything, awed by the company she found herself in. The pub named the Lamb and Flag proved to be just off Garrick Street. It was a pleasant, old-fashioned place which she judged was frequented mostly by the theater crowd. Everyone seemed to know Augustus Gordon and deferred to him. The star marched along proudly with her at his side as they were led to an excellent table in the privacy of a corner.

When they were seated he gave her an amused look across the table. He said, "I wonder that your father didn't get you some introductions to theater managers. I find it odd that you should be turning up at a public audition."

Ruefully she said, "Father doesn't want me to have a professional acting career."

The black eyebrows arched a trifle higher. "And you are determined that you will have one?"

"Yes."

"I might have guessed it," Augustus Gordon said. "You have the air of a rebel. A quiet one, but a rebel just the same!"

She smiled. "You believe you can read character?"

"It's part of my business," he said confidently as he studied the menu. "Just as it will be part of yours."

"I suppose you're right."

He eyed her over the menu. "And don't think the theater is going to be all that easy. You wouldn't have had a chance today if Jane Brady hadn't spoken for you."

This upset her. "You mean I wasn't hired for my talent?"

"You were," Agustus Gordon hastened to say. "But there were many others in that audition crowd equally gifted. We picked you out because we had heard about you. Acting is a risky, overcrowded profession, and your father was thinking of your good when he discouraged you from wanting a theater career."

She said, "Yet here I am. Ready to appear in a Terence Rattigan play with you in the West End. A pretty good start, isn't it?"

He gave her a droll look. "Not bad. Not bad at all." And then he added, "I don't know what you like, but my choice will be the veal cutlets. They do them superbly here."

Vanessa went along with his choice, and the luncheon was excellent. Since she was living in London on a budget, she had eaten in only the most modest places. To

14

her, the pub they were in represented elegance.

Over the meal, Augustus Gordon became philosophical. He told her, "I'm playing a titled gentleman in this play. And if I had my wish, that is what I would have been in real life."

She looked up from her plate. "Wouldn't you have found it boring?"

"Not at all," the handsome star said. "I would be active on the boards of various companies. Then there would be the directorships in charity foundations. And I would own horses and become part of that world. No, I'd have not the slightest difficulty in keeping busy. Especially if I had a compatible wife with a similar background."

Vanessa decided to be daring. She said, "You've already had three marriages, if I remember correctly, and none of them lasted."

He shrugged. "Blame it on the theater and blame it on my wives. None of them were the right sort for me. They were all actresses. Actors and actresses should never marry each other. They should find their mates outside the profession, where there can be no jealousies of a professional nature."

Vanessa's green eyes held a teasing look. "So you will never marry an actress again?"

"I didn't say that," the star protested at once. "I only say I would be wiser not to."

"I should think you'd be especially satisfied with your life," she said. "You are at the top of your profession."

He gave her another of his knowing looks. "The top is where you fall most easily. My life-style costs me a great deal of money. And there is the alimony I'm still paying. I can't afford to fail in anything I undertake. Film offers have not been coming my way so frequently lately, so it is especially important that this play be a success.''

''I'm certain it will be,'' she said.

''We shall see,'' the handsome if rather dissipated-looking Augustus Gordon said.

And happily the next few weeks proved Vanessa right. The rehearsals went along excellently. The director knew his work, and the actors from the star down fitted their parts. Vanessa felt she was in seventh heaven. She moved from her dingy room to a nicer one closer to the theater. And she was given a more important role to understudy. This added to her interest in the play.

Also, her friendship with Augustus Gordon continued. The older man seemed to enjoy her freshness and enthusiasm. Vanessa guessed that there must be many whispered speculations about her and the star, but she didn't care. She was delighted with his interest in her, and she sincerely tried to be honest with him. He asked her opinions about a number of things, and she did her best to be helpful.

There was a glamorous opening night, with the theater filled with celebrities. Vanessa was not too nervous, and enormously happy. And when she found the small bouquet of violets in her dressing room with a warm note of good wishes from her father attached to it, she shed tears of joy.

Jane Brady, the pleasant, middle-aged wardrobe woman who was also Mary's mother, came by to give her words of encouragement. The older woman said, ''Your part is small, but you do it very well. I'll guarantee you get a hand on your exit.''

''I doubt that,'' she said.

''I think you will,'' Jane Brady assured her. ''I've been

watching your scene at rehearsals. And so has Augustus Gordon.''

''Has he, really?''

Jane Brady smiled. ''You know, he has an eye for you, my dear. But in this case, it's strictly professional. Anyway, good luck.''

Vanessa was fine until she stood in the wings for her entrance. Then all at once the feelings of nervousness which she hadn't known earlier came to crowd in on her in a crushing way. Her hands perspired, and she felt her throat go dry. She didn't think she could go on! Next her cue came, and she marched out on stage. Within a matter of seconds a miracle occurred. She forgot all her fears in her absorption with playing her part.

Toward the end of her short but rewarding scene, she really began to enjoy herself. And when she made her exit, she did receive a small round of applause. Just as Jane Brady had predicted!

When the curtain finally came down on the opening performance and Augustus Gordon had taken his last bow, he turned to the company and said, ''Sir Edward Norville is giving us a party at Quaglino's. You are all invited!''

There was a happy reaction to this, and then Augustus Gordon left the side of his leading lady to stride over to Vanessa and take her hands in his.

Smiling, he said, ''You did beautifully! You must have heard the applause on your exit?''

''Modest,'' she said somewhat shyly.

''You earned it,'' the star said earnestly. ''I was wrong when I told you any one of those other girls who applied could have done as well. You have a special gift. With experience, you can be a star.''

Her eyes shone with happiness as she told him, ''My

17

father sent me his good wishes and violets.''

"Not enough," Augustus Gordon said. "Tomorrow night you shall have roses in your dressing room. And they shall be from me. You're attending the party?''

"Yes.''

"As soon as you've changed, meet me at the stage door," the star said. "You can go in my car. I have room for one extra.''

This meant she would be riding with Augustus Gordon and his female co-star in the play and the second woman in the company, whose role she was understudying.

She rushed off to her dressing room, pausing only to speak to the tall Harrison Hobbs, who had excelled in his butler role. She told him, "You were wonderful!''

The tall, thin man said, "And so were you! The play will run at least a year or two!''

"I hope so," she said, and then ran on upstairs to change.

While she was changing, the wardrobe mistress came by again. Jane Brady's broad face was glowing with pleasure. "I couldn't be more pleased if it had been Mary onstage tonight. You did so well, and they applauded you, just as I said they would!''

Vanessa glanced up at the older woman with a smile. "I know! I'm so thrilled! Augustus Gordon congratulated me, and I'm going to the party in his car.''

Jane Brady looked wise. "Trust Gus Gordon to spot a winner! You know, you could play Lady to his Lord for keeps if you gave it half a try.''

"I wonder," she said. "But then, I think he might change in his feelings about me. Jealousy in the theater is so common. If I marry—and I don't think I will for ages, since I want a career—I'd rather marry someone out of the theater. Perhaps a genuine title!''

The wardrobe mistress chuckled. ''You are ambitious!''

''Why not?'' Vanessa asked as she daubed a final spot of powder to her nose. Then she put on the necklace with its golden Capricorn sign that was her best piece of jewelry.

Jane Brady asked, ''Are you a Capricorn?''

''Yes,'' she said, rising. ''Why?''

''Nothing,'' the wardrobe mistress said. ''Only, that explains your ambition. Your Saturn influence is showing, dear.''

Vanessa thought no more about this. She quickly made her way down to the stage door, where Augustus Gordon's chauffeur was waiting for her. He escorted her out to the big gray Mercedes in the alley, and in a few minutes they were on their way through the busy streets of the neon-lighted theater district. Augustus Gordon had arranged it so he was seated next to her.

In the shadows of the car, he confided, ''Sir Edward Norville, who is having this party for us, is my best friend. He lives the sort of life I would like.''

She smiled. ''The titled member of the gentry!''

''Yes. I don't mind saying I envy him. But he's a good fellow, and I value his friendship. It's a nice gesture, his giving us this party. But then, he can well afford it.''

The party was held in a private room of the attractive nightclub. Almost immediately Augustus Gordon introduced her to the host. He was a year or two younger than the star, and in his own way just as good-looking. In fact, his squarish face had more character than that of the actor, and his blond hair and serious gray eyes combined to make an appealing countenance.

19

Sir Edward Norville held her hand for a moment longer than she expected. His gray eyes looked into hers as he said, "You are extremely beautiful, and you were excellent in your part."

She smiled. "A very tiny part!"

The blond man said, "I'm certain you'll soon be doing longer ones, and equally as well."

"Thank you," she said, blushing with embarrassment that he had singled her out to give her so much time.

He said, "I understand you and Gus are good friends."

"He has been kind to me."

Sir Edward Norville glanced across the room, where the star was in earnest conversation with his leading lady. The titled young man warned her with a wise smile, "Be wary of him! He has a way of sweeping young women off their feet."

"So I've heard," she said lightly. "I'm sure it won't happen to me."

"Probably not," Sir Edward Norville said. Then his eyes suddenly fixed on the necklace she was wearing. The young man's manner underwent a subtle but still noticeable change. And in an almost taut manner he asked her, "Are you a Capricorn?"

Chapter Two

Someone was playing a popular show tune on a piano in the background. There were murmurs of conversation and occasional bursts of laughter. A number of the guests were lined up at the buffet table with plates in their hands, and others were still having drinks as they stood scattered about in groups. She and Sir Edward Norville were facing each other close by the entrance to the big paneled room with its ornate cut-glass chandelier.

A trifle startled, she gazed into his suddenly shadowed face and said, "Yes. I was born a Capricorn. That is why my father gave me this necklace."

"I see," he said, still staring at it.

"Are you interested in astrology?" she asked.

The blond man with the handsome squarish face seemed all at once to change moods again. Now he was again his smiling self. "Not really," he said. "I merely noticed that the necklace was unusual."

"I'm rather fond of it," she said. "It was also my mother's birth sign."

"Then you do dabble in astrology," he suggested.

"I know something about it," she agreed. "But I wouldn't call it a main interest."

"You are new to the London stage," he said.

"Yes. This is my first West End show," she agreed.

He smiled. "I'm certain we're going to see more of you. You were excellent tonight. I hope we'll meet again."

"I hope so," she said.

"You will excuse me if I see to my other guests," he apologized. And he left her to cross to the buffet table.

Vanessa was left standing alone for a moment and feeling puzzled. She found it hard to understand why the young man had behaved so oddly at the sight of her Capricorn necklace. And there was no question that he had reacted to it. Yet he had denied being interested in astrology. So why had it bothered him?

She was asking herself these questions when the tall, thin Harrison Hobbs, who specialized in playing butlers, came up to her, wearing his usual solemn expression. He glanced in the direction of their host and said, "I see you've made the acquaintance of Sir Edward."

"Yes."

"Very much the man-about-town," the tall, thin actor said dryly. "He and Augustus Gordon go about together a great deal."

"I understand they are good friends," Vanessa said.

"Sir Edward is the last of his line. They have Norville House in Blake Square. Have you met him before?"

"Not until just now," she said. "Is he immensely wealthy, along with the title?"

"Sir Edward is not one of your poor baronets," Harrison Hobbs intoned in his solemn manner. "His family is very rich and dates back to the Middle Ages."

"You seem to know all about him," she said.

"I read the society news regularly," the actor who mostly played butlers said. "A hobby of mine. Sir Edward

22

lives at home with his widowed mother. His Uncle James, a judge, is also a member of the household, along with his wife and his son, who is about Edward's age.''

"Sir Edward is not married?"

"Not yet," Harrison Hobbs said. "But he is engaged to a neighbor's daughter, Lady Madeline Smith. Very pretty girl, by the way. She owns several racing horses, as does Sir Edward.''

She smiled. "That completes the picture. The sport of kings.''

"Sir Edward has done very well. He had a winner at the Queen's Cup races last year.''

"Thanks for filling me in so well on him,'' she said.

"Nothing at all,'' the tall, thin actor said. "There is some sort of legend or story about his family, which escapes me at the moment. But he is a colorful chap. You're liable to see him backstage a lot. He and Augustus are close friends.''

"So I've been given to understand,'' she agreed.

At that time one of the other girls in the cast came over to her, and after a moment of conversation they both joined the line for food. It was not until almost an hour later that she had a chance to chat alone with Augustus Gordon.

The star was in a good mood. Smiling at her, he said, "Well, how do you like all this?''

"Fantastic!'' she exclaimed. And with a knowing look, she said, "When you told me that you thought you would enjoy living the life of a titled gentleman, it didn't occur to me that you had so good a model in your friend. Sir Edward lives exactly as you described, even to owning horses and racing them.''

He shrugged. "I was only dreaming. I shall always be a

poor player of parts, like your father. But for us it is enough. We choose our roles in life, so why not be satisfied with them?''

"I'm glad to hear you talk like that," she said.

He glanced around at their host, who was chatting with the leading lady of the company. Then he asked her, "How do you like Edward?''

"He seems very nice.''

"He is very nice," the star assured her. "We have been close friends for the last five years. Ever since I returned from America.''

She said, "He has never been in the theater?''

"No." The handsome star smiled. "He is well able to fill his days with his duties as a noble of the realm. Not to mention the time he gives to his stables.''

"I'd like to see a big race someday," she said. "I've never been to one.''

Augustus Gordon said, "We'll have to correct that. I think Edward has an entry in the race next week. I'll check. If it's not on a matinee day, I'll take you.''

She gave a rueful smile. "From now on, I shall be a prisoner of matinee afternoons. I hadn't thought about that.''

"You'd better," the star told her. "We're likely in for a long run. I think the critics will give us good notices, and the audience seemed to have a wonderful time.''

"It's almost too good to be true," Vanessa said.

At this point it was the star's turn to notice her necklace. He took the Capricorn ornament in his fingers and studied it. "I didn't notice this before. Your birth sign?''

"Yes," she said. "And don't tell me you might have guessed, or I shall hate you.''

Augustus Gordon offered her one of his droll smiles as

he released the ornament. He said, "Did Sir Edward notice it?"

"Yes," she said, suddenly puzzled again. "He did notice it, and he reacted in a strange way. Does he have something against Capricorns?"

"I wouldn't say so," the star said. "But there is a story to it. I haven't time to go into it now. I'm sure he'll tell you one day, if you ask him."

She stared at the sophisticated Augustus Gordon. "Why do you make so much mystery of it?"

"I didn't mean to," he apologized. "When you are ready to leave, I'll be glad to drop you off at your place. We mustn't have my new discovery running about the dark streets of London after midnight."

"There's no need to worry," she said. "I can get a cab."

"Wouldn't dream of it," the star said. "We'll all be leaving shortly."

A few minutes later she paid her respects to Sir Edward Norville before leaving. She told the blond man, "It was a lovely party."

"You helped make it so," the young baronet said, holding her hand again. "I look forward to meeting you very soon."

"Augustus has promised to take me to see your horse race if it isn't on a matinee day," she said.

"Excellent," the young man said. "Be sure to look me up if you attend."

So it was almost settled when she would see him again before she left his party that night. In the interval before the day of the race, she was too busy adjusting to her new success in the theater to give much thought to anything else. Her father came down from Stratford one afternoon when they were both free, and they had lunch together. He was full of good advice for her.

"Don't think all your roles in the theater will come as easily as this one did," he warned her.

"I know that," she said.

"And it will not necessarily follow that every part you do will suit you as well as this one. You still have a lot to learn."

"I couldn't agree with you more," she told him as they had this final discussion at the entrance to the railway station.

Her father leaned forward and kissed her. "But I am proud of you, and I do think you're off to a good start!"

She watched him stride into the station and vanish in the crowd with a touch of sadness. It was one of the penalties of the profession they'd each chosen that they could not be together more. And she was terribly fond of her father. It seemed that all the love she would have had for both parents was concentrated in him, with her mother dead. Again the thought of death came to her and sent a chill down her spine.

It was stupid of her to be thinking of death and fearing it as she walked along this crowded street, but she could not help it. Along with her burning ambition, there was a wide streak of moodiness in her makeup—something over which she seemed to have no control. Her mother's death had shocked her when she was at a tender age. And the scars still remained to torment her. She told herself she must fight these feelings and concentrate on the present and her career.

The play continued to draw capacity audiences. On the Wednesday matinee, Augustus Gordon took her aside

26

after the performance and said, "We have a date for lunch tomorrow."

Her eyes widened with pleasure. "It's the first I've heard about it."

"You have a wicked memory," he rebuked her. "Surely you remember promising to go see Edward's horse race the night of the party?"

"Oh, that?" she remembered. "Of course I'd like to go."

"Then the proper thing is to have an early lunch in town and drive out to the track. The drive will take thirty minutes or so. Suppose I come by for you in my car around twelve?"

"I'll be ready," she said. "I'm looking forward to it. And to meeting your friend again."

The star showed a bored interest. "Really? I seem to recall his inquiring about you. It would seem you two are going to be friends."

"I'd enjoy that," she said.

The following noon she and Augustus Gordon had lunch at the Savoy, and Augustus told her about the race. He said, "Today we're going to Epsom. That's where the derby is run, you know."

"How late in the year does the racing go on?" she asked.

"Until next month," the star said. "It always ends in late November. Though there are steeplechase races held during all the year except in high summer."

"I know so little about it," she said. "But it appeals to me."

As usual, Augustus seemed mildly amused by her enthusiasm. He said, "Of course you'll enjoy it. Edward

27

has a mare in the fourth race, Flying Anne. I understand she is a favorite.''

"A favorite?''

"A favorite to win, my dear,'' the star explained.

"The terms are new to me.''

"You'll soon get on to them,'' he said. "Luckily we have a fine, sunny day. It can be coolish in the stands in late October.''

They drove out to Epsom, and she was amazed by the heavy traffic and throngs of people at the famous race-track. The noise and confusion were new to her. Augustus Gordon steered her through the crowd as they headed for the grandstand. The scene was picturesque, with the bookies and their tote boards, the gypsies, the toffs in their finery, and sinister-looking types who seemed straight out of the London underworld.

"Here's a character,'' the star said laughingly, and he hesitated a moment before a bookmaker sporting an enormous ostrich feather and decked out in fantastic regalia, including a patch of the Stars and Stripes. "He's Prince Monolulu, one of the best-known bookmakers in the business. Want to put something on Flying Anne to win?''

"Why not?'' she said gaily. And she drew a pound note out of her purse and gave it to the star to place for her.

When he finished the transaction, he came back and said, "The best I could manage was even odds. Flying Anne is a good mare.''

"It doesn't matter,'' she said happily. "I just wanted to feel part of it.''

Augustus guided her on, saying, "We'll see Edward after the races. Just now he'll be busy.''

"I'm sure of that,'' she agreed. "It would be like

having someone call on us a few minutes before the curtain was due to go up."

"Exactly," the star said. He made a dapper appearance in his heavy brown tweeds, with a tweed hat to match. And he carried binoculars on his shoulder for their use in following the horses.

They found their seats, which were high enough to see well but still close enough to the track to be able to make their way to the stables easily later on. The first race began almost at once, and Vanessa was thrilled by it.

She turned to Augustus and said, "This is spectacular! You have the open air and the excitement of the races! I'm sorry I didn't discover it long ago."

He gave a mock groan. "I was afraid you were going to turn out an addict."

"Not really. But it is fun."

"I agree," he said. And he passed her the binoculars to see the horses lining up for the second race.

It was a fairly long while before the fourth race was scheduled. But as the horses and their jockeys appeared, the star pointed out the chestnut mare owned by Sir Edward Norville. He said, "That's Flying Anne!"

"A beautiful mare!" she said, studying it through her glasses. "And I know nothing about racehorses."

"She's graceful and a favorite," Augustus Gordon agreed. "The chances are she'll win. Though she has raced in the rain and lost. Mud seems to make her nervous."

"There's no mud today," Vanessa said excitedly. "I think she'll win. How much will I get from the bookie if she does?"

"A pound to match the one you put up," the star said. "You were lucky to get even odds."

The race began, and the crowd in the grandstands soon were on their feet shouting their favorites along. Vanessa was caught up in the excitement and did as much cheering as the rest of them. Augustus Gordon followed the race with the binoculars, as he was more experienced, and kept her informed.

"Flying Anne is second," he announced.

"She must do better than that!"

"She's pulling ahead a little!"

"She must," Vanessa implored.

"Now she's taking first place," he said, unable to hide his own excitement.

"Good girl!"

"She's keeping ahead! She's heading on, with the others two lengths behind! She's winning!"

Vanessa screamed out the mare's name happily and added, "I knew she'd do it! I knew she would!"

Augustus Gordon was laughing at her. "Edward will be glad to know you took so much pleasure in his mare winning. And I don't think I've enjoyed a race so for years!"

"Can we go down now and see Edward and the mare?" she asked eagerly.

"Why not?" the star asked. "It's the moment we've been waiting for."

They located Sir Edward Norville at the stables, talking to his trainer. He at once came over and greeted them. A special look was exchanged between the young nobleman and Vanessa as they shook hands. He said, "I'm delighted you were here to witness Flying Anne's victory."

"I've never been before," she confessed. "I'm thrilled."

Edward smiled and said, "Come and meet the winner."

She followed him over to where the mare was standing with her proud jockey at her side. Flying Anne regarded her with some nervousness, but the happy jockey urged her, "Give her a pat on the nose, miss. She won't mind."

"You're sure?" Vanessa said, and she warily patted the mare's damp head. The pleasant, tangy odor of the perspiring animal filled her nostrils as she stood close to it.

Augustus Gordon showed his usual benign amusement, telling the young nobleman, "I think you have a dovotee here!"

"I should hope so," Edward said. "We'll all go to the club for a drink and celebrate. I'm meeting Madeline there."

Vanessa heard this with interest and recalled that the actor, Harrison Hobbs had told her Edward was engaged to a Lady Madeline Smith who lived next door to the family home in Blake Square. She wondered what this Madeline would be like.

And she soon found out when they went to the club built beneath the huge grandstand. They had barely sat down at the table when a fantastically pretty girl with a model's perfect features and body and long tresses of auburn hair came to join them.

Edward introduced them, and Madeline Smith showed a marked interest in Augustus Gordon and a much milder curiosity about her.

The titled young beauty told Augustus, "I've seen your play. It's excellent, and you are at your best in it."

Augustus smiled. "Thank you," he said. And he glanced at Vanessa and added, "Then you must also have seen Miss Masters. She has the part of the heroine's friend. Just one scene, but she does it well.''

Lady Madeline Smith considered and then told Vanessa, ''I do think I remember you. You were on toward the end of the second act.''

Vanessa nodded. ''Yes. It's just a bit.''

''Contributes a lot to the play,'' Edward said with a special look of friendliness for her.

Lady Madeline Smith offered no further comment on this, but turned the conversation to a discussion of the race. She had great faith in Flying Anne and thought the mare's future depended entirely on the races in which she was entered. In most of this conversation the titled young woman either deliberately or by accident ignored Vanessa.

When they left Edward and Madeline at the racetrack club and began the drive back to London, Augustus Gordon told Vanessa, ''I think Lady Madeline Smith is jealous of you.''

She gave the actor a shocked look. ''How could she be?''

He smiled knowingly. ''She understands Edward better than almost anyone. And I'm sure she sensed that he has more than a passing interest in you.''

''Then she senses more than I have,'' Vanessa protested.

Augustus Gordon said, ''I think Madeline is right to regard you as a rival. I also believe Edward is falling in love with you. And let me warn you against him.''

Vanessa was shocked by the star's words. She said, ''You have to be making fun of me! How could Edward be in love with me? We've only met a few times! And why do you feel you have to warn me against him?''

"One question at a time."

"All right! Answer me!"

The actor seemed to be considering what he'd say before he told her, "Sir Edward Norville is an impulsive young man. And he's used to getting what he wants. It is not impossible that he has decided he wants you."

"So?"

"So you'd better be cautious with him," Augustus Gordon warned her. "I think you have a great future in the theater. A marriage with him would sidetrack you."

"Why should it? Many girls who marry continue their stage and screen careers."

"You won't if you marry Edward Norville. He wouldn't like you to continue acting. More importantly, his blue-blooded family would be against it."

"Is that why you warn me against him?"

"One of the reasons," the star admitted. "The other is a rather different matter. I won't go into it now. You'd probably scoff at what I might say. But I think it might be actually dangerous to both you and Edward if you decided to marry him."

She stared at the man on the car seat beside her. "You really haven't told me anything. Just mentioned some vague threat. I'm afraid I can't take your warning seriously."

"You will disregard it at your own risk," the star told her in his assured way.

Little more was said on the drive back to London. Indeed, the subject was not discussed by them again. But Augustus Gordon proved to be a better prophet than she'd given him credit for. Almost immediately she began receiving flowers and gifts from Sir Edward Norville at the theater. And it was inevitable that she should begin dating the young nobleman more than she dated Augustus Gordon.

If the star was annoyed at this, he did not show it, even though he had warned her against becoming too friendly with Sir Edward. After a few weeks Edward spoke frankly to her. They were at Churchill's for a midnight supper after the show. In the dark, secluded corner of the famous nightclub the young man of title confessed his feelings for her.

"I love you, Vanessa," he said. "I want to marry you."

She stared at him in wonder. "Augustus Gordon said you would propose to me."

The blond man shrugged. "I can't imagine how he knew. But I do want you to be my wife."

"Augustus warned me about that as well. He thinks I ought to refuse you."

"Augustus is my best friend! Why should he say a thing like that?" Edward wanted to know.

"I suppose because he knows how ambitious I am. I'm just starting in the theater. I'd like to stay with it until I'm a star."

"You could be an old woman by that time. Don't you also want a husband and family?"

"Only if my husband will allow me to go on with my stage career. How would you feel about that?"

The handsome blond man eyed her earnestly. "I also am aware of your great talent," he said. "I'd have no objection to your working in show business after a period of time. I think you should interrupt your career for a year or two so that you would first be adjusted to our way of life. Then go back to the theater."

"The delay could be fatal. I'm very ambitious."

Edward shook his head. "With your talent, there is no need to worry. A year is only twelve months! Getting accustomed to being the new mistress of Norville House would take you that long. The months would pass very quickly."

"What about children?"

"I can wait for heirs," he said. "We're both young enough not to be in a great hurry."

She gave him a searching look. "One other thing. What about your family?"

"I do not live by their judgments," he assured her.

She frowned. "There must be something else. Augustus Gordon was very vague about it. But he suggested we might be bad for each other. What could he have meant?"

"I have no idea," the young baronet said with a slight hint of anger in his tone. "I can only think that he is in love with you himself, and so he's trying to discourage your considering me."

"What about Lady Madeline Smith?"

"I've already told her I'm in love with you."

"And?"

"We've broken our engagement. It wasn't going to work, in any event. It was a match desired by our families and not by us."

Vanessa gave him one of her beguiling, wistful smiles. "You overcome all my objections, make it sound so reasonable and possible. What can I say?"

"Say you love me and will marry me," Edward told her as he bent near to kiss her.

The next day she received a gigantic diamond from him. The first thing she did was go to Augustus Gordon's dressing room and show the ring to him.

The famous star groaned and told her, "Why did you have to do this before curtain time? I shall give a rotten performance tonight!"

Her eyes widened. "I thought you'd be happy for me!"

"You knew better! Little vixen with your Saturn ambitions! You've really gone and done it, haven't you?"

"Edward has promised not to interfere with my career," she argued.

Augustus Gordon stood up, impressive in his makeup and stage clothes for the role of Lord Darlingford. He gazed down at her sadly. "I tried to warn you! But I knew from the start you wouldn't listen. His promises won't mean much after you marry him. And it could be that your life won't count for much either!"

She stared at the star with concern. "What can you mean by that?"

"Ask Edward," Augustus Gordon said almost coldly. "He's the only one you listen to, in any event! Now, I have to rush to get onstage. I have no more time to discuss the matter."

This proved to be the attitude of the star in the weeks that followed. While he was pleasant enough to her, she was sure that he did all he could to avoid her.

It made a great change in the atmosphere backstage for her. If Sir Edward Norville hadn't been constant in his attentions to her, she would have been most unhappy. But the young baronet was at the stage door almost every night to take her out on the town, and he spoiled her with gifts. It was inevitable that several of the London society columnists linked their name in a number of stories about their nightclub adventures.

One night while they were dancing at the Dorchester the blond Edward said wryly, "That item in the *Mirror* on

Tuesday really did it! My family insist on meeting you. And I've been trying to spare you the ordeal as long as I could."

They were doing a slow, romantic number, and she looked up at him and asked, "Are you worried that they won't approve of me?"

"Not at all!" he exclaimed. "Whatever gave you that idea?"

"Then why worry about it?" Vanessa said. "I can visit them Sunday if you like. It's my only free evening."

"Fine!" Edward said, as they continued dancing. "I'll make all the arrangements. Mother enjoys entertaining. You shall be the guest of honor."

As the days went by, she became more excited at the prospect of meeting the rest of the Norvilles. She hoped she wouldn't be too unfavorably compared to the pretty Lady Madeline Smith. She had not heard anything from Edward about that titled young lady of late. Nor had they met her at any of the various clubs.

Edward was to pick her up promptly at six on Sunday evening. Drinks were to be served at Norville House at six-thirty, with dinner at seven-thirty. Only the members of the family were to be present, and she was sure she would be under cold scrutiny.

Her first hint that Edward was nervous came when he arrived at her lodging place. He looked uneasy when she came downstairs, but at once showed relief when he saw she was wearing a quiet gray woolen suit under her fur-trimmed coat of the same shade.

The handsome Edward gave her an approving eye. "I like your choice of outfit. It will fit in with the others. And you'll be glad you're wearing a suit, as Norville House can be a bit drafty."

She smiled mockingly. "I spared you anything shocking."

He was studying her closely as he said, "By the way, you haven't that necklace on, have you? The one you wear so often—with the Capricorn charm?"

Surprised that he should ask such a question, she said, "No. Why do you ask?"

"No special reason," he said. "I just don't fancy it would go well with that suit."

"And I had no idea you were planning to supervise my dressing," she said. "I'm not sure that I like it."

"Come, now," the young baronet said good-naturedly. "It's only that I want you to make an excellent impression."

Vanessa tossed her head with mock arrogance. "You have it all wrong!" she said. "It is they who must make their mark with me!"

He laughed. "Of course!" And he kissed her warmly before they went downstairs to his car.

When she had her first glimpse of Blake Square and the great Georgian graystone owned by Edward and his family, she felt just a trifle upset. It was all too grand and staid! Blake Square stood apart from the rest of London with quiet, tree-sheltered elegance.

There were no more than a half-dozen houses located around the square, and the largest and most elegant was Norville House. She saw a smaller house on its right and guessed this must be the residence of the Smiths.

She asked Edward as he brought the car to a halt. "Is that where Lady Madeline Smith lives?"

He glanced in the direction of the smaller house and nodded. "Yes. When she's at home. She's been away in the United States for a few weeks."

"So that's why we haven't seen her!"

Edward opened the car door for her. "I suppose so. Not that I'm anxious to meet her. It will be easier after we're married."

"Will it?" she said, not entirely sure what he meant.

He took her by the arm as they mounted the gray-granite steps leading to the regal entrance of Norville House. "Built by my great-grandfather," he said cheerfully. "I understand the Prince Regent was a frequent visitor here. He and my ancestor had a common taste for gambling."

"I have stage fright!" she whispered to him. "Suddenly I realize that all this and you are a terrific gamble for me!"

"Stop it!" he ordered her as he rang the entrance bell.

The door was opened by a pompous-looking man in a butler's uniform who wasn't anything like the tall, thin Harrison Hobbs at all. This man, whom Edward called Norris, looked like a bald, polite version of Sir John Gielgud.

And with Gielgud precision, he announced, "Lady Norville and the others are already gathering in the living room awaiting your arrival, sir."

"Thank you, Norris," Edward said warmly as the butler took her coat and then his and vanished with them.

Edward guided her into the great living room, with its walnut paneled walls, beamed ceiling, and huge crystal chandelier. With its rich antique furnishing, crimson Persian carpets, and fine oil paintings, it looked exactly like the stage set for a play of another century.

And assembled at the far end of the room before a huge fireplace of black marble, dominated by an enormous painting above it, were the various members of Edward's family, like the cast for the play. Vanessa almost giggled nervously at the thought she was making her entrance and would soon have her moment under the spotlight.

Edward took her directly to his mother, a large, stern-looking woman with a regal air and pure white hair. She was seated stiffly in a high-backed chair and wore a simple brown dress with a cameo at the breast. She studied Vanessa for a moment and then in a pleasant low voice said, "So you are the young woman of whom my son has told me so much!"

"I'm happy to meet you, Lady Norville," she said timidly.

Edward quickly wheeled her around and said, "And this is my Aunt Edith!"

Aunt Edith was tall, hollow-cheeked, and looked older than Edward's mother. She had an arrogant expression and thin lips. She spoke in a rasping voice, "I believe you are in the theater?"

"Of course, she is, Edith," a big, overweight man with a hearty voice and smiling, good-natured face said, coming to his wife's side. "I'm James Norville, Edward's uncle. And I've seen you in the play with Augustus Gordon! Excellent!"

"Thank you," she said, feeling she at least had him as a friend.

"Uncle James is a theater fan," Edward said. "Now, meet his son, my cousin, Leonard."

She turned to Leonard with a slight smile. And he was somewhat of a surprise to her. Though he must have been about Edward's age, he was not in the least like him. Leonard Norville was tall and thin, like his mother. He wore his hair at shoulder length, and it was a dull brown in shade. His thin face had a sullen expression, and there was

40

an uneasiness about his eyes. When he offered her his hand, she found it dampish.

"Welcome to Norville House, Vanessa," he said in a rather high-pitched, effeminate voice.

"Thank you," she said. "The house is so huge and elegant, I find it overwhelming." She glanced up at the portrait above the fireplace and saw it was of a lovely auburn-haired woman of the late sixteenth century. "And what a beautiful face that woman has!"

From her chair Lady Norville looked grim. "Lovely faces can be destroyed by evil," she said in a sharp tone. "She was one who learned that hard lesson. The first of the Brides of Saturn."

Vanessa found herself staring at the older woman and asking, "Who were the Brides of Saturn?"

Edward spoke up too loudly, saying, "Nothing! An old legend! You wouldn't be interested in it!"

And she was shocked to see there was absolute fear in his handsome young face.

Chapter Three

Edward's startling show of fear caused an immediate reaction in her. She was suddenly the poised young woman of the theater able to take her place on this new stage. She had the unhappy feeling that there was some very strong reason for her husband-to-be behaving as he had. And she was now determined to find out what it might be.

She met Edward's gaze directly and said, "On the contrary! I'm interested in the legend. I'd like to hear about it."

Despair showed in Edward's face as he shrugged and said, "It's not all that important!"

His uncle, Judge James Norville, showed mild amusement as he spoke up in his hearty way, "I'm delighted that Vanessa is interested in the family history. And I can think of no reason why we shouldn't tell her the story."

Leonard Norville looked bored as he confided in her, "Father fancies himself as a yarn spinner. Let me get you a drink first."

"Thank you," she said. "Whiskey and soda." And as the young man crossed to the sideboard to pour it for her, she turned to Lady Norville and went on, "Edward has really told me very little about his family."

"I can understand that," Lady Norville said in her cold

43

fashion. "He has been equally skimpy in his information about you."

Leonard came back with her drink, and with a smile on his thin, sallow face said, "I've seen your play. I admired the setting. Done by Gilbert. He's a good man."

His mother, Edith, said in her dry voice, "Leonard is an artist. That is why he is interested in scene design. Just now he's doing abstracts in his studio in Soho."

"How interesting," Vanessa said politely.

"I haven't lived here for three years," Leonard said with a hint of pride in his effeminate voice. He seemed uncomfortable in his smartly cut Edwardian-type brown suit. She imagined he would be a lot happier in sweater and dungarees.

Edward said, "He had a show last year, and several of the papers covered it."

The long-haired young man scowled. "The reviews were dreadful!"

Judge Norville cleared his throat. "Criticism is always a subjective thing," he said in his hearty way. "No need to let bad comments make one downcast." He raised his eyes to the painting of the young woman again and continued, "But you were asking about her. The first of the Brides of Saturn."

"Yes, I was," she said clearly.

The stout man cleared his throat again. "This painting came from our estate in Sussex. That is where the family really established itself. The Norville line began there. We have many ancient manuscripts dating back to that period. And it is from them that we learned the history of those days." He gave her a frank look. "Some of the history is dark stuff! Very dark!"

"Those were days of violence," Vanessa volunteered.

44

"We are much more violent today!" Lady Norville snapped from her chair. "We accept our own brutality and scorn that of the past."

The judge's ruddy face showed a tolerant look. He told his sister-in-law, "I think you lack the historian's point of view, Deborah. Our concept of violence is much different from the one held in those days."

Lady Norville eyed him in her cold fashion. "Murders are still murders!"

The stout judge coughed. "This is so," he said. And he turned his attention to Vanessa. "But you have asked me about the painting."

"Yes," she said, wondering why there was so much talk before dealing with it.

Looking thoroughly unhappy, Edward said, "I really think it can wait until after dinner."

"I'm liable to forget about it by then," his uncle said, and he addressed himself to Vanessa once more. "The young woman you see in the portrait was Mary, the second Lady Norville. She died a cruel death. Her body was found in her bedchamber one night. She'd been strangled by some person or persons unknown."

Leonard Norville showed a mocking look on his sallow face. "Come, Father! There was no mystery about who did it."

The stout judge gave his son a reproving glance. "I'm coming to that." And he told Vanessa, "You see, my dear, the second Lord Norville was a rake. One of his indiscreet alliances was with a maid in his mother's employ. Legend has it that she was a beautiful girl. He was still a bachelor, and she came to the mistaken conclusion that he planned to marry her. In the words of the manuscript describing the events, 'she found herself with child.

45

And on learning of his disinterest in her plight, hanged herself in a closet off his mother's chambers.' I'm quoting the original manuscript."

"Where does Lady Mary fit in the story?" Vanessa wanted to know.

"I'm coming to that," the judge said. "A few months after the maid's suicide, Lord Norville found himself a bride. The bride was Mary, daughter of one of the other landed gentry in the area. They were ideally happy in the beginning, and then one stormy night when her husband was away somewhere, Lady Mary was visited by an ancient, haglike woman."

"This is the part I like," Leonard Norville interrupted.

His father gave him a look to silence him and went on, "This old woman had the reputation of being a witch. She surely looked like one. She was the grandmother of the maid who had hanged herself for love of Lord Norville. And as she stood in the shadowed bedroom that stormy night, she pointed a bony finger at Lady Mary and pronounced a curse on her."

Vanessa found herself strangely caught up in the drama of long ago. "What sort of curse?"

"Lady Mary was born in January. The old woman called a curse on her head, and on the heads of all succeeding brides of the Norville family who might be born in January. That is when the curse of the Brides of Saturn began."

She heard this in disbelief. "You surely don't take a thing like that seriously?"

Edward's mother spoke up and said, "Tell her what followed."

"Yes, tell me," she said in a taut voice, aware of the

worry on Edward's face and the taut silence of the others.

Judge Norville gave a deep sigh. "Lady Mary was inclined to scoff at the curse. But when her husband returned, he showed his concern. And one of the things he did was have this fine portrait of his lovely wife painted. It was fortunate that he did."

"Why?" Vanessa asked in a strained voice.

"She shortly gave birth to a son," the old judge said with a frown on his ruddy face. "And weeks later she came down with the plague. She had to be sent to a distant wing of the old castle and kept from everyone. A genius of a family physician and good nursing brought her through the ordeal, but her beauty was ruined forever. Her face was covered with deep pockmarks."

"It was the curse!" Lady Norville said sternly.

Her brother-in-law sighed again. "People put it down to the curse. Her life was not a happy one following her illness. She gave birth to another son and a daughter, which ensured the line. But her husband was openly unfaithful to her and broke her heart. Then one night she was found strangled in her bedchamber."

Vanessa asked, "And they didn't know who the criminal was?"

"They put it down to the curse," Judge James Norville said lamely.

His artist son Leonard gave a sour laugh. "Why don't you tell her all of it, Father? Tell her that the whispers were that the second Lord Norville killed Mary when she reproached him for his unfaithfulness!"

"It was never proven," his father replied irritably.

The long-haired Leonard said, "Nor could they find any sign of anyone having entered the house. So it had to be one of the household or the ghost of that avenging old

47

witch. It was more convenient to blame the strangling on the witch.''

Judge Norville said, ''This became one of the dark happenings in our family history, of which I spoke.'' He gazed up at the wistful face of the long-dead young woman in the portrait. ''The portrait has a grim story attached to it.''

Vanessa asked him, ''What about the curse?''

Edward's mother spoke up, ''The family have always taken it seriously. And on those occasions when we haven't, there have been other violent deaths of Norville brides.''

Edward gave her an angry look. ''You're being too dramatic, Mother. In only two other cases over a period of two centuries have there been what might be construed as tragedies.''

Lady Norville gave her son a sharp eye. ''Two other Lord Norvilles married Capricorn brides, and in each case those brides died mysteriously and violently.''

The stout judge nodded solemnly. ''That's quite correct. One toppled off a high balcony; the other was burned to death in a fire of mysterious origin.''

His wife, Edith, sniffed. ''So it's not much wonder that when a Norville seeks a wife he tries to avoid one born in the month of January!''

''Ridiculous as it may seem, we believe there is something to the legend,'' the Judge agreed.

There was an awkward moment of silence in which Edward gazed with pleading eyes at Vanessa. She knew he was only too aware of her habit of frankness and was silently entreating her not to say anything. She was both angry and sorry for him, so she stood there without a word.

Leonard's mocking smile indicated that he thought the whole thing was hilarious. He said, "You wouldn't expect to find such superstition in this fashionable corner of London. Now, in Soho we have witches and curses galore."

Lady Deborah Norville gave him a crushing glance. "We know only too well the creatures you have in Soho, Leonard. And we do not care to hear about them."

Leonard looked abashed, and his father and mother lapsed into a moody silence. It was Edward who came to the rescue of the awkward moment by saying, "If we've all finished our drinks, I can think of no reason for putting off dinner any longer."

This suggestion met with general approval, and they all moved on to the dining room. Vanessa felt a slight relief in getting away from the portrait. The fine painting now had a frightening effect on her. She wanted to avoid it and forget the story connected with it. And above all, she was grateful that no one had asked her the month in which she'd been born. She didn't dare try to imagine what consternation the news she was a Capricorn would have brought to Edward's family circle.

The dining room proved to be as large and splendid as the living room. It also was a museum of fine furniture, rich oil paintings, and other suitably elegant appointments. She found herself seated next to Edward. But she really was lost in her own troubled thoughts all during the meal, so that the table repartee and the fine foods were wasted on her.

When the meal ended, Edward rather desperately announced that he wished to take her on a tour of the old mansion. And it was through this device that she finally found herself alone with him in a book-lined study on the second floor. Edward at once took her in his arms and kissed her.

He said, "I'm sorry about all that nonsense downstairs."

She looked up at him. "You mean the thing about the curse?"

"Yes."

"They didn't seem to think it nonsense."

Edward swept the air with an impatient movement of his hand. "They live dull lives. They like to draw on the past for their excitement. Even so silly a legend as the curse helps break the monotony for them."

Her eyes met his. "Tell me one thing, Edward."

"What?"

"How many Capricorn brides of your family lived happily ever after?"

He shrugged. "What does it matter?"

"Tell me!" she insisted.

He paused for a moment and then admitted, "None. But I still don't believe in the curse."

She smiled wryly. "Because at the moment you don't wish to. I know now why you didn't want me to wear my necklace."

Edward's handsome face showed embarrassment. "All right! I'll admit it. I felt it better for you not to wear that thing. It would have led to questions."

"And they would have found out I was born in January."

"Yes."

"And you don't want them to know?"

"Not yet."

"Not ever," she said, reproaching him. "But don't you see that is hopeless? They are bound to find out."

50

"We'll be married by then," Edward told her. "And we'll let them see that the curse doesn't work."

Her eyes met his as she asked evenly, "Suppose it does?"

Edward seemed shocked. "You can't really take that old wives' tale seriously?"

"I don't know what to think," she said. "But I'm sure they all believe it. With the possible exception of your cousin, Leonard."

"Leonard!" he said with disgust. "You can see the sort he is. And you're right, he doesn't believe the legend."

"Your mother does, and so do your Uncle James and Aunt Edith," she said. "What will they say when they find out?"

"Nothing," he said. "We love each other, and I don't intend to allow a silly old legend to come between us."

She smiled at him bleakly. "It's easy for you to be brave. After all, the brides are the ones who die violently!"

Edward said, "You didn't hear all the story. Almost without exception the husbands have also met their deaths mysteriously within a few months of their Capricorn brides' dying."

She sighed. "We've been too happy. I might have known there would be something!"

He took her hands in his and studied her solemnly. "You're not going to allow a silly old legend to stop us from marrying. We'll destroy the curse in our generation. It will be a service to the family."

"I don't know," she said, still unconvinced.

"Let us see some of the house," he insisted. "I told them we were taking a tour." He guided her through the upper floors, and she realized how vast the great mansion

51

was. The attic floor had been shut off to save heat and expense. It was now used only for storage.

He showed her the kitchen and the servants' quarters on the lower floor of the mansion at the rear. She met the bald and polite Norris once again. And he introduced her to the cook, Mrs. Higgins. The butler explained with some pride that he and Mrs. Higgins had been in service to the family for more than a third of a century.

Edward saved the cellars for the last. He led her down a broad stone stairway to a dark, dungeonlike area in which packing crates and other storage items seemed to be set out haphazardly. He had a strong flashlight, which he used to supplement the rather weak yellow light offered by bulbs suspended from the ceiling of the cellar at fairly long intervals.

She kept close to him in the shadowed, menacing atmosphere of the deep cellar. He told her, "I'm showing you down here because it is one of the most interesting parts of the house. There are claims that the cellar here has secret tunnels that connect it with the cellars of other houses in the area. And they also say there is a passage leading directly to a huge maze of tunnels under the city. I can't say for sure, for I have never found any of them."

"It is a very old house," she said, pressing close to him as fear of the place began to reach her.

"It is," he said. "After the Sussex estate burned down, the family came here—about a hundred and seventy years ago. The house was built to order for my ancestor. By the way, he was a connoisseur of wine, and so we have a fine, large wine cellar."

He guided her through the near-darkness to the locked door of the wine cellar, which was screened off from the rest of the area by wire walls. He explained that this was a recent improvement, as the original walls had become rotted. The dampness of the place had eaten into the wooden walls and destroyed them. He moved the flashlight beam over the rows of dusty bottles stacked as high as the ceiling. "We have wines to last for years," he said. "And we supplement the stock every season."

She gave a tiny shudder. "It is very damp down here," she said. "And I think I can hear water running in the distance. Could that be from the underground sewer?"

"I doubt it," he said. "There is some rather primitive plumbing down here. It could be some leaking faucet or something of that sort you're hearing." He glanced down at her. "You're not enjoying this?"

"Not too much," she admitted in a small voice, keeping close to him.

"Then let us go back upstairs," he said. "They'll be starting to wonder about us."

"Edward," she said pleadingly, "don't make me stay long. I want to get away."

"If you like," the young man said in a troubled voice. "But I must say it doesn't sound as if you are going to like the place or my people."

"I don't know yet," she said in a choked voice. "Don't rush me, Edward! I can't make up my mind until I think about it all."

"I say you're thinking about it too much," he protested as they made their way along the hard earthen floor of the ancient shadowed cellar on their way to the stairs.

Then, without warning, it happened. There was an eerie kind of screeching sound, the flutter of dusty wings, and into the beam of the flashlight a large bat came flying. She screamed as it came directly toward her, its fetid cold fur brushing her cheek.

Edward uttered a curse and swiped at the bat with the flashlight. By this time it had vanished into the blackness. He turned to her with alarm.

"Are you all right?" he asked.

She was trembling and feeling physically nauseated. She nodded. "Yes," she said in a whisper.

"Stupid creature!" he complained. "They're blind! It came straight at us!"

"Straight at me!"

"I'm sorry," he said. "But as long as it didn't hurt you . . . I have no idea how it got down here. No doubt there are passages leading outside, and it got in that way."

"Edward!" she said in a stunned tone.

"Yes?"

She gave him an awed look. "I think it was an omen. An evil omen. A warning."

"Stop!" he said. "I don't want to hear that sort of talk." And he hurried her on upstairs.

He was considerate in that he didn't require her to stay long talking to the others. When he drove her home, he talked about everything else but the old mansion and its occupants. He told her of a growing problem he was having at the stables. One of the trainers had come under suspicion when several of his best horses had performed badly at important races. Edward feared the trainer had been doping the horses and was trying to get evidence to prove this. But it wasn't easy, and in the meanwhile he had to keep the fellow in his employ.

"I know he's a bad one," Edward complained. "But I have to try to let him trap himself."

"Aren't you afraid he'll do more harm?" she asked.

"A chance I have to take," he told her.

At the door of her lodging place his kiss was tender, and

he held her in his arms for a long while. As he let her go, he said, ''Nothing must part us. We must not let anything come between us.''

She nodded a wordless assent, as she was too mixed up and depressed to make a reply. As she mounted the stairs to her room, she realized that she had just visited a different world. This other world had none of the glitter and glamour of the theater. It was all too real! Its people thought differently and had very different values. If she entered it, she would be a stranger for a long while.

As she prepared for bed, she thought about the curse of the Brides of Saturn. She considered that she had outgrown a belief in such things long ago. But had she? For all her ambition and courage, there was still a moody, self-destructive side to her nature. She had always been aware of this and fought it. But now she worried whether she would be strong enough to stand up to the Norvilles and their family curse.

It was not surprising that she had nightmares that night, and on many of the nights that followed. In her nightmares she was always in that damp and dark old cellar being pursued by a witchlike creature. Forever fleeing from this threatening phantom. Several times she awoke in a cold sweat and lay staring into the darkness, filled with a fear the like of which she had never known before.

And it was inevitable that her fears also shadowed her days as well as her nights. When she was with Edward she tried to avoid any discussion of his family or the mansion, and so a new tension came between them. Some of her carefree manner deserted her, and of course it did not take Augustus Gordon long to notice this. The star was perceptive, and he at once sensed she was not happy.

He began to give her more attention, and one evening

after the show he invited her out for a late supper with him. She was not seeing Edward on this particular night, so she thought it might be wise for her to accept the invitation. She needed someone to talk to, and her father was away in America on tour. Augustus Gordon was the only one she had to turn to.

When they were seated at the restaurant table over drinks, he told her, "I've noticed a change in you lately, Vanessa. What is wrong?"

She sighed and stared down at the table. "I guess I'm worried."

"About what?"

Vanessa lifted her eyes to look directly at the star. "Do you believe in family legends? Curses that follow down through the years?"

Augustus Gordon said, "You're thinking of the curse of the Brides of Saturn, aren't you?"

Her eyebrows raised. "How do you happen to know about it?"

He smiled wearily. "Come, now! Edward and I are old and close friends. I knew him years before you came along. I was bound to hear of the family curse."

"I'm sorry," she said. "I forgot."

"So now you know about it. Did you tell the Norvilles you are a Capricorn?"

Vanessa's cheeks warmed. "No," she said quietly. "Edward asked me not to."

"I can well understand why," the actor said. "He knows his family will raise a storm if they think he's going to defy the curse by marrying a Capricorn."

"Edward doesn't put any stock in the curse."

"Too bad the others are so superstitious!"

"What do you think?"

56

The famous actor grimaced. "I have been against your making this marriage from the start."

"I know."

"The Norvilles won't want you in the theater, and you'll never be happy away from it," he warned her.

"Edward has promised me I can resume acting within a reasonable time," she insisted.

Augustus gave her a scoffing look. "You think he means it? Or even if he does, do you imagine he can stand up to that stern mother of his, or the others?"

"I'd hope so."

"So do I, but he won't," the star told her. "And as if that isn't bad enough, you'd also be flouting the legend. You ask me if I think it is valid? Frankly, I don't know. But I have read a history of the Norvilles, and every January bride has died a violent death, and often their husbands as well. Why are you and Edward so sure you can break the chain of evil?"

"He thinks we can," she said faintly, knowing that it sounded far from convincing.

The star showed disgust. "He is so madly in love with you, he'll say anything. You are the one who must keep your wits about you. Do you want to risk it?"

Her eyes blurred with tears, and her lips trembled as she protested, "I love him!"

Augustus regarded her unhappily. "In a way, I feel I am to blame for all this. I brought you two together."

"You had no idea how things would turn out."

"No," the star said frankly. "As a matter of fact, I've wanted to marry you myself."

She stared at him in surprise. "You?"

"Yes? Why not? I'm only five or six years older than Edward. The fact I've had unhappy marriages before makes people think I'm older than I am."

Vanessa said, "I've always counted on you as my friend, but I had no idea you were seriously interested in me."

"You know now."

She shook her head. "You're only trying to help me. It wouldn't really work."

"Why not give it a try? We can star together in a series of plays. The stage is what you really want! And I represent the stage. Edward will try to end your career."

"I don't think so."

"Wait and see," Augustus Gordon warned her. "Why not solve the whole unhappy business by saying you'll be my wife?"

"Let's not talk about it any more."

"If that's what you want," the handsome star said. "But do think about it. And believe that I mean my offer."

She gave him a wan smile. "I do, Gus. And thank you. I'm truly flattered."

He stared across the table at her with a wry smile. "But it's Edward you love and want to marry."

It was the beginning of a difficult time for her. She and Edward saw a lot of each other, and yet some of the original happiness she'd known in their relationship seemed to be missing. The young baronet was in a troubled state about the problems in his stables. His horses continued to have a losing streak, and he'd not yet been able to gather enough evidence to make criminal charges against the trainer.

When they were out walking one afternoon following a visit to the races, she glanced at him and said, "Maybe

I'm to blame for this problem your're having with your trainer."

He showed surprise. "What do you mean?"

She shrugged. "The curse. Maybe it has begun to work since we plan to marry."

"Nonsense!"

"Why shouldn't it? We are engaged. We've set the date for our marriage."

"That's just foolishness," Edward said, a trifle too irritably.

"I wonder," she said.

"I'm in trouble because I have a crooked trainer doping my horses, and so far I haven't been able to catch him at it. It's as simple as that," he said.

"I'm sure the family would blame it on me," she said. "And by the way, when are you going to tell them I am to be another Capricorn bride?"

He frowned slightly. "I'm not sure it is any of their business."

She said, "I promise you, they'll think that it is."

"Do you insist I tell them?"

"Yes."

"Very well. I will."

"When?" she asked.

He was slow in replying. Finally he said, "Give me a day or two."

"Take a week if you wish," she told him. "But it must be done. Just remember that."

"I will," he said, his tone irritable again.

The subject was dropped, but to the best of her knowledge he didn't tell his family about her birthdate. Nor did he even mention it again. She continued seeing him, and kept hoping that somehow it would all turn out well.

Augustus Gordon made an effort to take her to lunch fairly often and to talk to her about it all. He told her, "I hear that Edward's horses aren't doing well."

They were seated in a small café near the theater that they often visited. She sighed and admitted, "They haven't been. But it will be better."

"I wonder," the star said with meaning.

She blushed and gave him a look of rebuke. "We decided not to discuss Edward or his doings."

"Your idea," the star said, "not mine. I'm waiting for you to give my offer some more thought."

"I don't want to discuss that either," she said.

The star smiled. "Then you won't mind my leaving you for a moment. I have an important phone call to make."

"Please, go ahead," she told him.

The famous stage star left her alone at the table while he went in search of a phone. Vanessa gazed around her, taking in the happenings in the busy restaurant, the people continually arriving and leaving. All at once a girl came directly across to her table and stood gazing down at her rather arrogantly.

"You don't remember me?" the girl in a brown suit with a red-fox stole at her throat said.

Vanessa got over her surprise and said, "I do now. You are Lady Madeline Smith. You were dressed differently, and your hair was longer when I saw you last."

"That was before I went to the United States," the auburn-haired girl said.

"Yes. I guess it was," she said rather uneasily.

Lady Madeline Smith's smile was not all that friendly.

In a cold tone she said, "And of course, since then you and Edward have become engaged."

"We have."

"It's a mistake," the girl brazenly told her. "You two will never be happy!"

Taken aback, Vanessa asked, "What makes you think that?"

The girl gave a small laugh. "You shouldn't give out interviews to the Sunday papers. You remember the story they did on you as the promising bit-part actress in the Augustus Gordon play? You told them your birthday was in January. You're a Capricorn!"

Vanessa suddenly remembered the interview and that she'd carelessly given out the information. It hadn't seemed important at the time. But Lady Madeline Smith had seen the story.

Before she could make any answer, Lady Madeline swept off to a table at the other side of the room. Vanessa was left feeling ill. Since the auburn-haired girl had seen the article, it was all too likely that some of Edward's family had also read it. It had been printed for all the world to see!

Augustus Gordon came back to the table. "I've made my call," he said, sitting down. Then he stared at her. "What in the world is the matter? You're white as a sheet!"

"Nothing, really," she protested. "I think it's because it is very warm in here." But she didn't think he believed her.

The next afternoon marked one of the last racing days at Epsom. Edward picked her up and drove her to the race-track. On the way, she asked him if his family had seen the article.

He nodded grimly. "I'm afraid so. Before I had a chance to tell them."

"I'm sorry," she said. "But I did warn you."

"I know," the handsome blond man said, his eyes on the road ahead as he drove in the thick traffic. "Well, perhaps it worked out better this way."

"What did they say?"

"The usual," he said bitterly. "I haven't paid any attention to them."

She settled down in her seat. "It sounds as if it was pretty bad."

"We'll talk about it after the race," he said.

They reached the track, and she went with him to the owners' stables. A youth came to greet Edward and told him, "Can't locate Mr. Hawkins anywhere. And Flying Anne is acting strange."

She listened to this news from the doleful-faced young stableman and knew that Hawkins was the trainer under suspicion. Now it seemed that he might have suddenly taken off, leaving Edward's prized horse in a bad state.

Edward looked shocked. "Will she be able to race?"

"I don't know, sir," the youth said. "The jockey is in there now. You'd better see. And watch out! She's very restless. Real wild, sir."

Edward turned to Vanessa, "Wait here a minute," he said, and left her abruptly without waiting for a reply.

She stood there tensely and watched him enter the stable. He hadn't been inside a moment when she heard the uproar of shouts and wild neighing, along with pounding hooves. The youth who had brought the bad news to Edward had been standing inside the stable with another youth. Now he came out and ran to her.

"It's Mr. Edward," he gasped. "The mare kicked him

and knocked him down. Pat is with him! I'll go get some help!''

Vanessa thought she would faint. She stood there frozen with fear, unaware of what was happening. All she could think of was the curse. And that all too swiftly it was striking them.

Chapter Four

The stableboy vanished in his race for help. Vanessa turned toward the open stable door and saw another, younger lad dragging out Edward. The sight of the man she loved unconscious and disheveled brought her out of her hysterical, rigid state. With a cry of distress she rushed forward to kneel by Edward and gaze down at his pale face. There was a deep cut on his cheek, which was bleeding profusely.

"Isn't there something we can do?" she asked despairingly as she touched her hankie to the wound to stay the flow of blood.

The lad, whose name was Pat, was also kneeling. He gave her a reassuring glance and said, "The doctor ought to be here in a minute. There's always one on duty."

"What happened?"

"The mare went wild," the lad with the freckled face and sandy hair said. "I think Hawkins must have tried to dope her, and something went wrong. Hawkins took off, and when Sir Edward went into the stables to try to calm Flying Anne, she kicked him and then tried to stomp on him. It was lucky we got him out of the way!"

Edward stirred slightly and opened his eyes. He stared up at her with a look of shock and fright on his white face. Then he asked, "What about the mare? Has someone gone for a vet?" He tried to sit up.

She pressed him down on the grass. "Don't try to get up! You're hurt! We don't know how badly!"

Edward groaned. "I'll be all right. Someone better see to Flying Anne before she harms herself. Damn that Hawkins for whatever he did! She'll have to be taken out of the race."

By this time a crowd was beginning to gather. From the stable came the restless neighing of Flying Anne and the uneasy pounding of her hooves. Vanessa heard voices and the sound of running footsteps. Almost immediately a jaunty middle-aged man in a houndstooth suit came and bent down over Edward.

"It's Dr. Benson," the man announced himself. "What happened to you?"

Edward tried to sit up and then fell back with a groan. He managed in a taut voice to say, "Something happened to my mare. She's gone mad. I think I have a cracked rib or two."

Dr. Benson nodded. "Most likely. The best thing for you is to get you to the nearest hospital. I've ordered an ambulance to come by and pick you up."

"Not an ambulance!" Edward protested.

"Best!" the doctor told him. "It will save time and pain for you. After you've had a good examination, we can decide what to do with you!"

Edward pleaded, "I can't just leave a situation like this."

Dr. Benson told him, "The mare will be taken care of. The boys are here to wait for the vet." And he turned to Vanessa and said, "You are with Sir Edward?"

"Yes. I'm his fiancée," she said.

"Fine," the doctor said briskly. "You can drive his car

to the hospital." And he told her where it was, just a few miles from the track.

Edward meanwhile was busy giving the boys instructions about the care of Flying Anne and where to contact him later with news about her. Before he finished, the screaming of an approaching siren announced the arrival of the ambulance. Two attendants jumped out and quickly put Edward on a stretcher and transferred him to the ambulance. Then it drove off, with Dr. Benson in the front seat beside the driver.

The vét had arrived and was busy attending to the mare. The boys had vanished to take part in the animal's treatment. The curiosity seekers had now wandered over to group around the stable door, and Vanessa found herself standing alone. She knew she had to keep her head. The first thing she must do was find the car, and she had only a vague idea where Edward had parked it. Bracing her shoulders, she headed for the big parking lot.

It was almost an hour later before she arrived at the hospital. She went directly to the emergency desk and was directed to a room far down a long corridor. Edward was sitting up in bed with his face bandaged, propped up by several pillows.

His face showed an expression of relief on seeing her. He said, "I've been worried about you!"

By his bedside, she said, "What about you?"

He grimaced. "I've been up for X rays. They found three ribs broken on the left side, and I'm all neatly strapped up. I don't think there is any other damage except bruises and cuts."

"There better not be!" she said. And she leaned close and kissed him.

Edward smiled after the kiss. "Better than the pain

tablets they've given me. I feel doped. Floating on a cloud with a vague ache on my left side. They want me to stay here overnight.''

"Naturally," she said.

His good-looking, squarish face showed distress. "I want to find out about the mare."

"She'll be all right, I'm sure. Once the vet gives her treatment for whatever that Hawkins drugged her with."

"Hawkins!" he said angrily. "I'll have the police on him!"

"You should! You could have been killed!"

"Or one of the stable lads could have been caught in the same trap," Edward said. "The mare was crazy. I've never seen an animal in such a state."

She said, "Once you suspected Hawkins, you should have gotten rid of him right away."

"I realize that now." He sighed.

"What about your mother?" she asked. "Have you let her know?"

"Not yet."

"You'd better," she warned. "Otherwise she might hear it on the television or radio."

The young man in bed gave her a worried look. "I know," he said. "I wish you'd do it for me."

She stared at him. "What?"

"Tell Mother," he said. "You have to go back to London. You have my car. You can leave it at my place. I'll take a taxi to town tomorrow."

Vanessa suddenly had an attack of nerves. She shook her head. "I don't think I'm up to it. Better that you phone her."

"No. Best that you do it," he said. "I have no phone here."

They argued for a few minutes, and she finally agreed, with a great deal of reluctance. He convinced her that she had to return to London to do her show and that it would be best for his mother to hear the news from her. Vanessa gave in to him, but she had grave doubts of the wisdom of the plan.

These doubts were justified an hour later when she sat in the impressive living room of Norville House facing the stern Lady Norville.

The atmosphere of the shadowed living room was grim.

Lady Norville listened to her coldly and then said, "In a way, I'm not at all surprised that this has happened."

"Really?" Vanessa said, baffled.

"No," Edward's mother said acidly. "And I don't think you should be, either. You know the tragic family legend, and you are a Capricorn."

"You read the article?"

"I did!"

Vanessa said, "I don't see that my being a Capricorn has anything to do with it. And if you're blaming it on the curse of the Brides of Saturn, you should remember that Edward and I are not married."

His mother snapped, "You're engaged!"

"That isn't the same."

"I question that," the older woman told her in her stern fashion. "Once you knew about the curse, I would have expected you to have the good sense to break with my son."

"Edward doesn't believe in the curse."

"Edward is oblivious of everything but his love for you," Lady Norville said. "I have tried to talk to him. So has James. But it has done no good. You are the one to put an end to the engagement."

Becoming more annoyed each moment, Vanessa rose as she said, "And if I choose not to?"

"Be ready for more of what happened today," the older woman said grimly. "Haven't you had lesson enough? Edward injured and in a hospital! Must one of you die before either of you see your folly?"

"I would rather not argue this with you," Vanessa said unhappily. "Edward asked me to bring you the news about him, and I have done so. Now I'll go."

Lady Norville rose grandly to her feet and pointed a finger at her imperiously. "You know that you came into Edward's life and upset a match with a fine girl! A girl who would have made a suitable wife for him!"

She could not refrain from saying bitterly, "Lady Madeline?"

"Yes, since you name her. Lady Madeline!"

Vanessa said, "She has already let me know about that. I'm afraid I'm not much interested. It is Edward who made his choice. Since I'm very much in love with him, I'm content with things as they are."

Lady Norville's wrath shadowed her stern features. She said, "If you come into this house as his bride, you will surely come under the curse."

"Is that a threat?"

"I'd prefer that you considered it a warning. You will be sealing your own doom and that of my son. I suggest you think it over again carefully before you make any rash decision."

Vanessa said, "I promised Edward I would let you know about his accident. I don't think we should discuss anything else."

"I see," the older woman said quietly. "Well, take your own course. If you come here as Edward's wife, I shall say no more about this, but you will understand how I feel."

"I will," Vanessa agreed grimly. "And now, I must leave, or I'll be late for the theater."

She hurried from Norville House as quickly as she could. Just outside Blake Square she found a taxi to take her to the Aldwych.

She managed to get through the performance somehow. But when it was over and she'd changed, the full impact of the thing hit her. She sat crying in her dressing room. It was there that Augustus Gordon came to find her. When he knocked on her dressing-room door, she dabbed her eyes with her hankie and called to him to enter.

The tall, handsome actor came in and took one look at her, then said, "You're not crying about Edward?"

She glanced up at him awkwardly. "No! He'll be all right."

"Then why?"

"It was his mother," she said. And she then proceeded to relate the unhappy meeting she'd had with the titled woman.

The actor shrugged and said, "You must have known you would run into something like that."

"I expected her to be more understanding."

"That's something you aren't apt to find at Norville House," he told her.

She frowned in disbelief. "They actually seem to believe in that old curse."

"Why not? Many people are superstitious. And this thing happening to Edward so soon after your engagement is bound to start the rumors again. Aren't you afraid for yourself?"

"I don't think so."

71

"Maybe you should be," he said.

Vanessa eyed him with surprise. "Are you that superstitious?"

He smiled grimly. "All actors are."

"I see it rather differently," was Vanessa's bitter reply. "I think she is trying to use the legend as an excuse to break my engagement to Edward. She wanted him to marry Lady Madeline."

Augustus Gordon said, "Maybe Edward's mother is right. You both might be happier if you gave up the idea of marrying. Madeline Smith would make Edward a suitable wife, and you have your career to think of."

"Just one thing wrong about that."

"What?"

"Edward and I love each other. We want to marry."

The handsome leading man spread his hands in resignation. "So neither of you will listen to reason?"

"I'm afraid not."

"I hope it isn't too bad for you."

"Thanks," she said dryly. She rose from her dressing-room chair, ready to leave.

Augustus Gordon smiled indulgently. "I'm still terribly fond of you, Vanessa, despite your stubborn streak. Can I see you home in my car? You must be tired."

"I won't refuse," she said with a faint smile. They left together, and he saw her home in the big limousine that came for him every night.

At her door he removed his hat and kissed her gently. "Don't worry too much," he said.

"I'll feel better when Edward is on his feet again."

"When will that be?"

"Tomorrow," she said. "He's planning to come back

to the city as soon as the doctors see him tomorrow morning.''

The handsome actor stood in the cool midnight darkness and suggested, ''Why not think about me, Vanessa? It's not too late yet.''

''Thank you,'' she said sincerely. ''I'm sorry.'' And she went inside and up to her room.

She did not sleep well that night. She dreamed about the accident, and she also had nightmares in which the legendary witch pursued her through dark-shadowed places once again. She woke up the following morning feeling depressed and worried. Around noon she had a phone call from Edward and at once felt better.

''Where are you calling from?'' she asked.

''Home,'' he said. ''Thanks for dropping by and telling mother. She appreciated it.''

''Did she?'' Vanessa asked over the phone. ''I wasn't all that sure yesterday.''

''Don't worry about it,'' Edward said quietly.

''What did the doctors say?''

''Just my ribs. They want me to take it easy for a day or two.''

''You should.''

''I will,'' he promised. ''The mare came around all right. But Hawkins has vanished. There's no doubt he was responsible.''

''What a mad thing for him to do,'' Vanessa said. ''He had a good job with you.''

''I understand he had been gambling and was heavily in debt. Apparently he had the idea that by doping some of my horses and fixing races he could get himself out of trouble. Instead, he likely plunged in deeper.''

''Better to be rid of him,'' she said.

"I intend to find him and settle with him," Edward said in an angry voice.

"When will I see you?" she asked.

"I'll come around after the show tonight."

She worried, "Are you well enough?"

"Of course! I may have some further news for you by then," he said.

After the conversation over the phone, she went out to do some shopping. It helped occupy her mind. She was strolling along a small side street on her way back home when she looked up and saw a sign, "Fortunes Read," painted in black letters on a plain white board. The sign extended on an iron rod from a building of ancient vintage. A cobbler's shop occupied the lower floor, and a narrow flight of dark stairs led up to the floors above.

Vanessa on sudden impulse decided to visit the fortune-teller. Clutching her various parcels to her, she began mounting the stairs. On the second floor a second sign indicated that the fortune-teller was on the floor above. Despite the meanness of the building and the fact that there seemed to be no one on this floor, she took the second flight of stairs to the upper regions of the old building.

At the head of the second flight of stairs she found herself facing a sign that read: "Madame Gina, Astrologer and Tea Cups Read. Ring the Bell." Dutifully she rang the bell and waited. After a very long time, in which she was able to note the smell of age and vintage boiled cabbage that hung in the hallway, there was the sound of heavy footsteps approaching and then the door was opened cautiously.

"Yes?" a female voice with a slight accent said from the shadows inside.

Vanessa replied to the hidden presence timidly, "I'd

like to have my fortune read.''

"Come right in, dearie," the hearty female voice with the accent said as the door was swung open to reveal one of the largest women Vanessa had ever seen. The woman was not tall, but immensely fat. She wore a kind of gypsy ornamental headdress and a loose-fitting gown of some dark material, which reached to the floor.

"I haven't very long," Vanessa said, already regretting she had given way to this impulse.

"Don't worry, dearie," the fat woman said in her warm way. "I don't waste time over my readings. I was slow about opening the door just now because I've been bothered by one of those collection-agency chaps. Real nasty sort who doesn't know his place. Coming around and threatening his betters!"

The fat woman closed the door and waddled ahead of Vanessa, leading her along a short hall to a room decorated with some drapes that had a lot of glittery material sewed to them and looked as if they might have been bought secondhand from some theatrical scenic supplier. The single table had a red-velvet cloth with a long fringe. And directly in the middle of the table sat a large crystal ball in a stand. A lone window overlooking an array of tenement rooftops and chimneys gave light to the small room.

Madame Gina waved Vanessa to one of the chairs at the table with a fat hand. "Put your parcels on the floor, dearie," she said.

Vanessa sat down and obeyed the woman, placing her parcels carefully on the carpet beside her. "You are an astrologer?" she asked.

Madame Gina nodded. Her many-chinned face was brownish in tone, and she had a serious expression in her large black eyes. "I give every kind of reading. What is your birthdate?"

"January," Vanessa said, and gave her the date.

The stout Madame Gina nodded approvingly. "I should have known from your strong white teeth and the way you handle yourself. You Capricorn women all have poise. But Saturn rules your passions and your secret wishes. You have problems of being sure of yourself, but once you've conquered them, you can learn to rule your world!"

Vanessa listened to this with interest. Madame Gina seemed to have a good deal of assurance of her own, once she embarked on her subject. She said, "I have come here with a special problem."

"Time to get around to that, dearie," Madame Gina said. "My fee is one pound in advance."

"Yes, of course," Vanessa said, and she found her purse and fumbled in it for a crisp one-pound note while Madame eyed her with avid interest. It began to worry Vanessa that she might have her purse stolen or her money taken from her in this dark, shabby place. Shakily she extended the banknote to the older woman.

Madame Gina snatched it eagerly and tucked it in her dress at the level of her ample bosom. She at once said, "It may take more than one session for me to help you. But we can begin today." It was obvious that she wanted to keep the flow of one-pound notes coming, once they began. Standing across from Vanessa at the table, she said, "I feel in the mood to read you in the crystal. Do you object?"

At this point Vanessa felt she wouldn't object to anything, just as long as she was able to emerge from the place safely. In a taut voice she said, "The crystal will do. But I can stay only a few minutes. I have a friend waiting for me.'' This was invention, but she hoped it would protect her.

Madame Gina offered no reaction to this information, but waddled to the window and drew some heavy drapes across it, which shut out nearly all the light. Then, breathing heavily, she sank down into the chair opposite Vanessa and turned on a switch somewhere under the table, which lit up the crystal ball and reflected an eerie glow on her huge moon face.

The fortune-teller said, ''When I'm in the mood, the crystal is the best of all!''

''Really?''

''And today I am in the mood,'' Madame Gina intoned as she gazed deeply into the crystal. ''You work before the public, don't you? Not a waitress! Not a clerk! I say you are an actress!''

It gave Vanessa a start that the woman should hit it so correctly. Then she began to wonder if the stout Madame Gina might not have seen her in the theater. But the fortune-teller did not seem a playgoing type.

Vanessa said quietly, ''You're right. I am an actress.''

Madame Gina was gazing into the crystal. ''There is a confusion. But I see a man. There is a man near you who loves you. I do not think you love him.''

''Go on.''

''It is cloudy,'' the stout woman grumbled. Then, after a slight pause she said, ''There is another man. A man with a shadow over him. He is the one you love.''

Tensely Vanessa asked, ''What sort of shadow?''

Madame Gina raised her eyes from the crystal and in a solemn voice said, ''I have no wish to frighten you.''

''Tell me!''

77

The face so weirdly lit by the crystal's glow was grim as she said dramatically, "The shadow I see is the shadow of death!"

"No!" Vanessa exclaimed.

"It is what I see."

"You must be wrong! Look again!"

"I will try." The old woman sighed. She gazed down into the depths of the lighted crystal once more. There was a taut silence in the room; then, after a long pause she said, "I see an old house. You are there. In great danger! It is part of that other shadow. You are alone!"

"What sort of danger?"

"Danger of death," Madame Gina said. "I see it for the man you love and for you. There is a third person as well, but it is all very cloudy. Perhaps another day!"

"No!" Vanessa protested. "You must try to see today!"

Madame Gina sighed again. "The crystal is completely clouded. There is nothing more for me to see. You should be cautious in your love affair. Turn away from this man, who will bring you nothing but sorrow. Marry the other man, who loves you."

"You have only confused and frightened me!" Vanessa complained.

"I'm sorry," Madame Gina said. "Maybe another day the crystal will be clear. Come back again." She snapped out the light under the crystal ball and rose heavily to waddle to the window and open the drapes. The light flooding into the small room was her signal that the session was over.

Vanessa picked up her parcels and purse and stood. In a small, troubled voice, she said, "Thank you."

Madame Gina had changed from solemn to cheerful

once again. "Don't be upset, dearie," was her advice. "Come back another day, and I'll probably be able to straighten it all out for you."

"Yes, I will," she said awkwardly, and headed for the hallway.

The stout Madame Gina waddled alongside her and opened the door and let her out. "Mind what I said about coming back," the old woman said. "Next time it will be better, dearie!"

Vanessa thanked her again and quickly descended the two flights of dark stairs to the street. Once on the sidewalk, she felt less nervous. But it had been an unsettling experience. The old woman seemed to have read her problems in the crystal with uncanny correctness. It was unbelievable that she could have hit it so accurately.

Walking briskly back home, she tried to convince herself that the stout Madame Gina was a harmless old fake. The big woman was clearly more interested in getting her pound-note fee than anything else. And the frightening information was a ruse to get her duped victims to come back to her. Vanessa told herself she had been silly ever to consult the fortune-teller in the first place.

Yet, in the back of her mind a new fear lingered. There had been something impressive in the old woman's manner as she gazed into the crystal ball. Was it possible that Madame Gina possessed the gift of reading minds? Had she read her mind and discovered all about the curse of the Brides of Saturn? It didn't seem likely. It was more plausible that the fortune-teller told every young woman who consulted her that two men were in love with her and she preferred one to the other. It was the expected thing. And didn't all people fear danger and death? Madame Gina was on safe ground.

Vanessa rested before going to the theater. She also tried to put the memory of her visit to the old fortune-teller out of her mind. That she wasn't quite able to do this was to be expected. But she did somehow get herself in a better mood before leaving for the theater. She knew that Capricorns were given to brooding, and it was something she had to fight against.

Augustus Gordon was entering the stage door just as she was, and he at once asked her about Edward. "How is he?"

"Better. He's coming by to pick me up tonight," she said with a small smile.

The actor raised his heavy, dark eyebrows. "That was a swift recovery."

"He hasn't completely recovered, but he's able to get around."

"So it would seem," the actor said dryly. "Tell him to stop by my dressing room and say hello. I haven't seen him for too long a time."

"I will," she promised.

Augustus Gordon gave her a searching glance as they headed for the dressing-room stairs. "You look wan," he told her.

"I was out shopping all afternoon."

"Take more rest," he told her. "When you're weary, it's bound to show in your performance."

She went on to her own dressing room and changed for the first act. While she was still seated and making up, Jane Brady, the wardrobe mistress, came into the dressing room and handed her an envelope. She said, "A young man came by and left this."

She took the envelope and saw her name written on it. "Do you know who it was?"

"Never saw him before," Jane said.

"What did he look like?"

Jane considered. "Thin young chap with longish hair."

She at once decided who it must have been. She said, "I think I know who it was." Hastily she tore open the envelope and read the message scrawled on a single page: "Don't give up the Norvilles! The curse is nonsense! Affectionately Yours, Leonard."

The wardrobe mistress said, "I promised to see you received it."

"It's from Sir Edward's cousin," Vanessa explained. "A very pleasant message. Thanks for bringing it to me."

The show went well, as usual. Edward arrived just after the curtain came down. He went up to her dressing room with her, and she showed him Leonard's note with a smile.

She said, "It seems I have one Norville admirer I can count on."

Edward read the message and then folded it and gave it back to her. He grimaced. "Leonard is bound to be all for you, as long as you upset the rest of the Norvilles."

She lifted an eyebrow. "And is that what I do?"

Edward looked apologetic. "You know what I mean. The others are worried about that curse thing. My accident yesterday convinced Mother that the curse is working against us."

"So she suggested to me."

"You mustn't mind her or Uncle James and Aunt Edith. They are old and set in their ideas."

"I'm well aware of that."

"The whole thing will be forgotten, once this business of my accident blows over," he assured her.

"I wonder," she said.

Edward took her in his arms. "There is no question of it!" He held her close and kissed her. Then he winced. "Sorry, my ribs aren't just right for embracing yet!"

Vanessa laughed lightly. "You'd do well to be careful. Augustus wants to see you. Why don't you go down and have a chat with him while I'm changing?"

"Good idea!" Edward said. "I want to talk to him."

They left the theater about a half-hour later, and Edward took her to the Royal Court Theater Club, which had become one of their favorite places. They sat side by side in a pleasantly intimate corner of the room and ordered a light supper.

As they lingered over drinks, Vanessa glanced at the young man beside her and said, "What did you and Gus talk about?"

He smiled. "Various things. He wanted to know all the details of the accident."

"And?"

"He always had the idea Hawkins wasn't to be trusted."

"Had he told you so before?"

Edward said, "He claims to have. I'm not all that certain. Anyhow, he was right."

"What else did you talk about?

"You," Edward said with a smile. "Gus thinks you are getting better as an actress all the time, and he pleaded with me not to make you leave the stage."

"What did you tell him?"

"That you'd desert it only temporarily. But that didn't seem to satisfy him."

"I know," she said, remembering her own discussions with him.

"We also planned to have a few nights on the town

82

together," Edward went on. "I miss seeing Gus. So one of these nights when you want to turn in early, I'll cover some of the old ground with him."

"I'm not sure I approve," she protested.

"Perfectly innocent," Edward told her. "Matter of making the rounds of the pubs and having a few drinks."

She said, "What about your mother? Is she still in a state?"

He frowned. "No. She was better as soon as she saw me and knew I hadn't been seriously hurt. She'll get over all that business."

"I wish I could be sure."

"You needn't worry!"

"But I do," she said. She gave him a troubled look. "What would have happened in the family if you'd been killed in that accident?"

He showed surprise. "What do you mean?"

"I mean, who would gain by it? Who would inherit the title and the estate?"

Edward said, "If we were married and had a son, my son would get the title. Or my daughter. The bulk of the estate would be in trust until he or she came of age, with you and our lawyers as guardians."

She insisted, "I'm not thinking of that. What if you had died yesterday?"

"I'm not sure," Edward said, surprising her.

"Not sure?"

"No."

"I'm afraid I don't understand," she said. "Surely you have a will of some sort."

Edward frowned. "In this case, my will has little bearing on the matter. Normally my Uncle James would come into the title and my share of the family fortune."

"The judge."

"Yes, as father's younger brother. And in turn, the title and estate would next go to Leonard."

"So Leonard would become Sir Leonard Norville."

Edward nodded. "But I'm not sure about it in this case. My father left a sealed envelope with his instructions of what he wished done in the case of my death without an heir."

"A sealed envelope?"

"Yes. In the event of my marriage, the envelope is to be destroyed without ever being opened."

She gave a tiny gasp. "That surely is mysterious!"

"My father enjoyed mysteries," Edward said lightly. "I don't think it is all that strange. Father liked to make a great deal out of the smallest things."

"So?"

"It is my idea that in his will he wished to skip Uncle James and have the title and estate go directly to Leonard. My father and Uncle James were not all that friendly."

"You hadn't told me that before," she said.

"It didn't come up."

"So you think that this sealed envelope would be to Leonard's benefit?"

"I'm almost positive of it."

Vanessa's lovely face shadowed. Her mind was working swiftly. She thought of Leonard's letter of encouragement. His warm wish that she continue in her plan to marry Edward. No wonder he wanted her to do this if he believed in the curse of the Brides of Saturn! It could mean he'd get the title and estate!

Chapter Five

She turned to Edward and asked him, "Just how friendly are you and Leonard?"

"We're really not friendly at all."

She frowned. "Then why was he so quick to send me a consoling message?"

"He probably likes you. Leonard is a strange person. Very much his own man."

"I'm beginning to believe that," she said. "He probably wants us to marry because I am a Capricorn. Likely he secretly believes in the curse and is waiting for the worst to happen, so he can get the title."

Edward looked shocked. "You don't really think that?"

"Why not?"

"Leonard isn't all that ambitious. He enjoys painting and Soho. Uncle James and Aunt Edith give him an allowance to live on. He's perfectly happy as long as they don't summon him to Norville House too often."

"I wonder."

"Why do you wonder?"

"People often have secret ambitions you never guess. Maybe Leonard secretly wants to step into your shoes."

"I'd say you were wrong."

"I hope so," she said. "Another thing. I wish you'd sell your stables before we marry."

Now Edward really registered shock. "Sell my horses?"

"Yes."

"You can't be serious!"

"I am!" she insisted.

"Why?"

"I'm afraid there may be other accidents like the one you had yesterday," she said.

"Not likely."

"You can't tell."

Edward looked uneasy. "I've never been injured before. Why should it happen again?"

"I have a strange feeling about it."

"Nonsense!" Edward protested.

"Look," she said seriously, "I went to a fortune-teller today. I know you're going to make fun of me. And maybe she was a cunning old fake. But she told me something that made my blood run cold. She claimed she saw you in the crystal, and there was a shadow of death over you!"

"Vanessa!" he said with reproach.

"An old woman who'd never seen me before," she went on in a nervous fashion. "She told me I was an actress and that you were in great danger. She told me all this, and knew only my date of birth!"

"These fortune-tellers are all fakes!" Edward said.

"I wonder."

"Now you're being worse than my mother," Edward said. "You must forget all about this nonsense. And all about the curse as well. The whole business is silly superstition, and you have to fix your mind on that!"

Their food arrived and interrupted their discussion. She

was sure that Edward was grateful for this. And she was also certain he was glad that the show followed shortly afterward and gave them no chance for any more serious talk.

But she forgot none of it. Madame Gina's words preyed on her mind, as did the legendary curse. Edward attempted to get her to visit Norville House several times, but on each occasion she found a reason to refuse. She had no wish to come under the cold scrutiny of his mother again, nor did she relish another meeting with Judge James Norville and the tight-lipped Edith.

Several weeks went by, and the weather became colder. There were a few inches of snow on the ground for a weekend, and then rain came to take it all away. But Christmas and the new year were only a few weeks ahead. The play continued successfully, and Vanessa saw a good deal of Edward, since the stables were closed for the season.

One week early in December he went to Liverpool to see about purchasing a gelding that had made a name for itself in northern racing. Vanessa missed him, since they were always in touch by phone on the rare days when they didn't meet. To make things more bleak, a heavy fog descended on London, and its yellow pea-soup mist lay thickly over the city for days and nights.

There were soon a number of empty seats in all the theaters because of the danger of getting about the city. Cars moved at a crawl, and in some cases patrolmen walked before the big buses with special lights.

Augustus Gordon sputtered, "The best season of the year for theater business, and we have to get a spell like this!"

Vanessa had her own problems. Getting to the theater

and back home became a hazardous journey each night. She couldn't get taxis, and so she had to walk. Cabs would have been of little benefit in any case.

The one bright ray in all this bleakness was a letter from her father in New York. He was playing there in one of the traveling Stratford productions, and it had taken the American city by storm. The company had meant to play a limited season of only a few weeks, but so great was their success that it had settled down to a run that would last for months at least.

"I shan't likely see you until the late spring," her father had written. "We'll be returning then for the new Stratford season. I hope you don't settle your marriage plans until my return. I have many things to discuss with you. It is rather surprising to me that you are considering marriage at all when you are doing so well in your stage career."

Vanessa read the letter from her beloved parent with a sad smile. Most of the time her father managed to misunderstand her. He had been the one most against her going into the theater, and now he was the one most determined that she should continue in show business.

She noted his reference to her marriage plans and felt quite secure in this. She could not see that Edward was planning on any early marriage. She hoped that he would at least wait until the end of the run of the play in which she was appearing with Augustus Gordon. She hated to give up the part that had won her so much attention.

Lately she'd tried to forget about the curse of the Brides of Saturn and everything else pertaining to the ghostly gray edifice of Norville House. All that would be something to deal with when the time came. Lady Norville had not sent her any direct invitations to visit the old mansion, for which Vanessa was grateful. She wondered if the cold Lady Norville and the imperious Lady Madeline Smith sometimes discussed her over tea.

The evening after she received her father's letter, the fog was as thick as ever. She ventured out into the weird, mist-enshrouded night and slowly headed toward the theater district. It was not all that easy. The newspapers were full of stories of people who had taken wrong turns in the fog and become completely lost. Vanessa had nightmares of this happening and of her being late for the theater.

Because of this, she left early and made her way along the foggy streets with great caution. It was amazing how the city was so weirdly transformed by the thick mist. Streetlamps and the headlamps of cars and buses became blurred and their beams cut to almost nothing. The windows of stores were bright only when you were close by them. Everything looked different.

She arrived at the theater safely. Once again there were many empty seats. And once again Augustus Gordon was in a rage about the one thing he could not do anything about, the weather! Vanessa had thought of asking him to take her out for a bite after the theater, since Edward was away, but seeing his black mood, she said nothing to him.

Getting back home was as much of an adventure as finding her way to the theater. As soon as she had changed, she hurried down the steep metal steps backstage to the stage door. The old man in charge tipped his cap to her as usual as she went out.

No sooner had she stepped out into the thick, wet fog of the alley than she felt a strong premonition of danger. It fairly surged through her. At first she felt she should rush back inside and wait for someone else to accompany her out into the shrouded street. But then she decided she would try to make it alone, though she was trembling with fright.

The alley was narrow, and there were no other doors or windows opening on it other than the stage door that she had just left. She picked her way along its cobblestone surface, still in a state of terror, when she heard the slight sound of movement from behind her. Someone stealthily slipping up close to her!

She screamed, and at the same instant of her crying out, cruel hands seized her. She struggled against her unknown attacker and screamed again. Now the hands transferred themselves to her throat! She felt the maniacal pressure slowly throttling her and tried to scratch out at her assailant. But as the steellike fingers tightened on her throat, she lost the ability to fight back.

Now all she could think of was managing a breath. She was on her knees, with her head back, as the murderous hands went about their work. She groped feebly at the hands with her own but could barely manage this last weak gesture of resistance. Then she blacked out completely.

"Vanessa!" She heard her name as from a long distance. Then it came again, hollow and ghostlike. "Vanessa!"

She opened her eyes and looked up into the face of Harrison Hobbs. The tall, gloomy-faced actor was kneeling over her. She looked around and saw that she was stretched out on the floor near the backstage door. The old backstage doorman was standing by with his pipe in one hand and his mouth open in shock.

Harrison Hobbs spoke to her again. "Vanessa! I thought you must be dead! I found you stretched out in the alley!"

Now it came rushing back to her. Memory of those

moments of terror. She gazed up at the character actor with frightened eyes. She reached up to touch her aching throat with her right hand and whispered, "Attacked!"

"I guessed that," Harrison Hobbs said impatiently. "I must have scared whoever it was away. I came out of the stage door and was groping my way down the alley in the thick fog when I stumbled upon you."

Vanessa's throat was paining her and making it difficult for her to speak. Again in a hoarse whisper she managed, "Came upon me! Tried to throttle me!"

"It's been a picnic for robbers since the fog settled on the city," Harrison Hobbs said. "But why should anyone want to choke you to death? Should've been enough to take your pocketbook!"

There were voices in the background, and then Augustus Gordon came upon the scene, dressed in topcoat and hat for the street. His handsome face took on an expression of concern as he saw her stretched out on the floor.

"Vanessa!" he exclaimed and knelt by her alongside the tall Harrison Hobbs. "What in blue blazes has happened?"

Harrison Hobbs answered for her. "Someone attacked her in the alley. Apparently to rob her, but they also tried to choke her to stop her screams!"

Distressed, the star said, "Help me take her to my dressing room." And he moved swiftly to lift her up by the arms, while the character actor took her by the feet.

"I'll be all right!" Vanessa protested, feeling embarrassed at being handled like a limp sandbag. By this time others of the company were crowding around and asking a lot of questions. The backstage area was suddenly a center of excitement.

Augustus Gordon's dressing room was on the stage

level, so it took only a few minutes to get there. Vanessa was coming around to herself more with every passing minute, and by the time they reached the privacy of the room, she was well enough to insist on sitting in the one easy chair there.

Augustus Gordon removed his hat and coat and studied her with concern. "You must have a doctor!"

She shook her head. "No! My throat is feeling better now. You'd never locate a doctor at this time of night."

The actor frowned. "There must be one available."

"I don't need one," she protested. "But I wish someone would look for my pocketbook!"

"I'll see about it!" veteran character actor Harrison Hobbs said, and hurried out of the dressing room.

Now she and Augustus Gordon were left alone. The star was clearly upset. He said, "You shouldn't have gone out in the fog alone!"

"I've been doing it nearly every night."

"I know. I've been too concerned with the slackness in box office to think of anything else," he apologized. "I've neglected you!"

"No!"

"I have," he insisted. "And I'm sure Edward will be angry at me for it."

She hadn't thought of Edward up until now. And she realized that he would be shocked by what had happened. She said, "We can worry about that later. Edward is in Liverpool for a few days."

"You're sure you don't want a doctor?"

"Quite sure!"

Augustus Gordon was pacing up and down impatiently. He said, "The police must be informed. And you should remain here until they come."

"All right."

"Did you get a look at your attacker?"

"No," she said, her aching throat making her speak in a husky fashion. "It happened too quickly!"

"That's too bad," the actor worried. "Even a brief look at him would have helped."

"I'm sorry."

"No wonder you didn't see him," Augustus Gordon said. "To be attacked as you were in the darkness and fog. You hadn't a chance."

"I tried to scream, and then he began to choke me," she said.

"Probably some petty crook who became frightened you'd attract the police," Augustus said.

There was a knock on the dressing-room door, and he went over and opened it. The stage manager was there with a uniformed policeman. The stage manager said, "I took the liberty of sending out for an officer."

At the door the star said, "You did right! Come in, officer. Miss Masters has a story to tell you."

The policeman removed his hat and took out a notebook and pencil, and standing before her, said, "If you'll just give me an account of what happened, miss."

Vanessa launched into her version of the attack, and he wrote it down without comment. By the time he'd finished, Harrison Hobbs had returned.

The character actor reported to Vanessa, "Not a sign of your pocketbook. I'm afraid it's gone for good!"

She said, "I'm not surprised."

"Nor am I, miss," the uniformed officer said. "We've been getting more than our share of these hit-and-run robberies since the fog closed in."

Augustus Gordon asked, "Why did the fellow have to half-kill her?"

"Afraid of her screams, I'd say," the officer ventured.

He asked Vanessa for a description of the pocketbook and its contents, which she provided. Then he took her name and address and promised to be in touch with her.

After he left, she stood up and said, "I'm well enough to go home now."

"I'll see you there safely," Augustus Gordon said. "And I am going to send out instructions that none of the ladies of the company are to leave the theater unescorted while this fog condition lasts."

The star was as good as his word. He saw her safely home in his limousine. The journey in the thick fog took three times as long as it should have. And before he left her, he promised to have his car drop by and take her to the theater the next evening.

It was not surprising that she had nightmares again that evening. Nor did it come as too much of a shock that her badly swollen throat gave her trouble the next day. She called the star at his apartment and in a croaking voice woefully told him her understudy would have to go on for a few performances.

Augustus Gordon's reaction to this was typical. He assured her not to worry, that her understudy would go on. And he at once arranged for a friend of his who was a specialist in throat problems to call on her at home. She was surprised and embarrassed when the eminent man came to see her.

The doctor smiled and told her, "Augustus has done me many favors over the years. And I never have to worry about tickets to his opening nights. They're always sent to me in the mail. So this is a small way in which I can repay him."

"I'm sure there was no need to call you," she said in her hoarse voice.

"You don't sound too good," the doctor said, opening his bag. "Let me take a look at you and try to find what is amiss."

"Just the bruises," she said.

And when he completed a thorough examination, he agreed with her. "As far as I can tell, there is no serious damage. I'll give you something to gargle, and in a few days you should have a normal voice again."

The doctor had barely left when a plainclothesman from the CID arrived to question her. He went over the same ground the officer had on the night before. But he asked her some other questions, which mildly surprised her.

The lean-faced inspector asked, "Have you any enemies, Miss Masters?"

She stared at him. Then she said, "None that I know about. Why?"

He sighed and frowned at his notebook. "We are assuming it was a straight robbery. And perhaps it was. But there is always the chance it might have been something else."

"Something else?" she asked in a startled voice.

He nodded. "A murder attempt by an enemy."

"I hadn't thought of that," she admitted.

"Well, do you have any ideas now?"

"No."

"There would have to be a motive for such an attack," the inspector went on in his grave, logical fashion. "You say you can't think of anyone who might have such a motive?"

She shook her head. "No. I'm afraid not."

"No one in the theater?"

She gave him an amazed look. "Of course not! How could you think of such a thing?"

"Members of the theater company and those working backstage would have the best chance of making the attack on you—other than some professional criminal who was deliberately lurking in the shadows waiting for a victim."

Vanessa clasped her hands tightly on her lap as she thought about this. Then she said, "It had to be a criminal from the outside. I'm sure I have no enemies in the company or backstage."

"I see," the inspector said. "Well, the pocketbook was taken. That indicates it was a robbery."

"So that gives you a motive," she suggested.

"It does," the inspector said, rising. "And I'm afraid I can't offer you much hope of getting back the pocketbook."

"There was very little money in it. But my keys and some private papers are missing."

The inspector said, "I'd advise you to have your door lock changed this very afternoon. And in due time get copies of your papers made, where it is possible."

She found herself feeling helpless. "I don't know where to find anyone to change the lock," she confessed.

"I have the number of an excellent firm not far from here," the inspector told her. "If you wish, I'll make a call and explain the urgency of the situation. I'm sure they'll send a man over before tonight."

"Please do look after it, inspector," she said gratefully.

Late in the afternoon the thick fog began to lift. The man from the locksmith arrived and went to work. She was relieved that the lock would be changed, since there was every chance that the criminal who had so ruthlessly attacked her might come to the building and try to rob it. Having the lock changed would guarantee her safety from this happening.

But the thief did have her address and might well lurk in the hallway of the building waiting for her to show up and then force his way inside. It wasn't a pleasant thought, and she began to worry about moving. But she liked her present location, and it would be difficult to find another place at the same price.

As she paced up and down waiting for the locksmith to complete his task, she thought of other things. She remembered that Madame Gina had looked into her crystal ball and predicted danger for her. And she had not dared to tell the inspector that she might be suffering from an ancient curse on the Norville family. The legend of the Brides of Saturn would have little interest to the matter-of-fact police minds. Yet she couldn't help wondering and worrying. Was it possible that the attack on her had come about as part of the curse?

An answer to this came from an entirely unexpected source. And it came before the day ended. The locksmith had been gone only a half-hour when she received a phone call. It was from young Sir Edward Norville. The man to whom she was engaged was in a troubled frame of mind.

"I've read about the attack on you in the evening paper," he announced over the line.

"Edward! I'm so glad you're back!" she told him.

"Your voice sounds badly off!"

"It's nothing serious," she replied. "A specialist has been here to see me. I'll be all right in a few days."

"You might have been killed!"

"Are you in London?" she asked, ignoring his comment.

"Yes," he said. "I got back an hour ago on the late-afternoon train. And a jolly good thing. Damn Augustus for allowing this to happen to you!"

"You can't blame him!" she protested.

"Why not? Allowing you to go out in that fog. They could as easily have found you dead in that alley as alive!"

"It's over!"

"Not as far as I'm concerned," Edward said tautly. "I'm going to pay Augustus a visit, and then I'm coming over to see you."

"Don't bother Augustus," she protested. "I'll be here waiting for you. My understudy is going on for the next few performances."

"I should hope so," Edward said grimly.

"Bring me the papers," she said. "I haven't seen them. What do they say?"

"You're spread all over the headlines. 'West End actress attacked.' They've made the most of it!" he said bitterly.

She put down the phone in a worried state of mind. Not only was Edward upset about what had happened to her, he was also annoyed by the publicity given the incident, knowing that his family were bound to read of the incident and probably find it another reason for disapproving of her. They had not been able to forgive his deserting Lady Madeline Smith for a mere actress. Now the actress had been indiscreet enough to have her name in the headlines! The fact that she had been the victim of a cruel attacker would make no difference to them.

Edward arrived at six and at once took her in his arms. After he had held her close for a few minutes, he led her to the divan by the fireplace. She had prepared a small wood fire to make it more comfortable. It seemed to her he looked very weary.

"I've talked with Augustus," he said.

"What did he say?"

"He admitted there was guilt on his part in allowing you

to go out in that fog alone. But admitting it makes little difference now.''

She said, ''I think the best thing is to forget all about it.''

The young man showed astonishment. ''You can do that after being almost killed by that fellow?''

''It won't do any good to dwell on it.''

''I'm glad you have such a healthy attitude,'' he said bitterly. He rose and began to pace in front of her. ''I'm afraid my family hasn't.''

She looked up at him. ''Does it concern your family?''

''They seem to think so,'' he said, halting his pacing. ''You are going to be my wife.''

''And?''

''Mother spoke to me about it the moment she saw me. She had read the story in the morning newspaper. She considers it another example of the Norville curse at work.''

Vanessa gasped. ''I wondered how long it would be before I heard that.''

He spread his hands. ''You must admit it fits in. Following so soon after my own accident.''

''How can they possibly link the two? Or consider my being attacked and robbed the result of the curse?''

His eyes met hers with a certain look of meaning in them. He said, ''That is the sort of thing which has been happening to the Brides of Saturn and their husbands over the years.''

Vanessa shook her head. ''You sound almost as if you believed it!''

''I don't know what to believe,'' he said bitterly. ''But I do know one thing. I don't want you around that theater any longer.''

She sprang to her feet. ''What are you saying?''

Edward came to her, and taking her by the arms, spoke to her earnestly. "I've discussed it with Augustus. Told him exactly how I feel. And he said it should be left to you."

"What?" she gasped.

"Whether you remain in the play or not."

"But of course I'll remain in the play. Why shouldn't I?"

"Because I want us to be married right away!" the blond Edward said.

"Right away?"

"Yes," he went on seriously. "I have it all planned. We will fly to New York and be married there in a civil service. I have friends there, and we can honeymoon right in the city."

Stunned by it all, she said, "But I'm not ready!"

"Your father is playing in New York, isn't he?" Edward asked. "It will mean he can attend the wedding."

She stared at him and then asked, "What about your mother and the rest of the family?"

The handsome Edward looked unhappy. "Mother would want us to wait for ages. Maybe try to have us put the marriage off altogether. I can't hope for her approval. The best thing is for us to elope."

Vanessa listened to him with mixed feelings. She said, "But we do have to come back to London. And to Norville House."

Somewhat taken aback by her saying this, he nodded. "Yes, we do. But it will be all right by then. You will be my wife."

With a bitter smile, she said, "Do you really think that will make any difference with your mother?"

"She will accept you more quickly this way," the

young man said earnestly. "Believe me, I know her."

"You're asking a good deal of me," Vanessa told him.

He nodded solemnly. "I know that. And I expect you to do as I ask, because you love me."

She heard him and wasn't properly able to think it all out. So much had happened in the past twenty-four hours, and now here was Edward sweeping her off her feet with a proposal that they elope. It would mean giving up her promising career, leaving the play she enjoyed, and beginning a new life. But it would also mean marrying the man she loved, having a chance to see New York and her father, and eventually returning to the stage with Edward's promised permission.

"Well?" Edward asked. "What is your answer?"

In a voice filled with tenderness, she replied, "You know it can only be yes."

The twenty-four hours that followed were like a mad sort of dream. Somehow she got together a suitable wardrobe and was ready when Edward came to take her to the airport. She burst into tears when she found a farewell party from the company at the airport, headed by Augustus Gordon.

The handsome star kissed her good-bye and told her, "I would feel worse about this if I weren't sure that in the end the stage will win out. If you have to desert Edward for it, you will!"

She laughed through her tears and asked him, "Can you forgive me for leaving the play?"

"Very easily," the star said. "The run is ending in mid-January, which is only a few weeks away. Since I've had an offer to do a film, we won't be touring. So you'll only miss the last two or three weeks."

"You've made me feel better!" she said, and kissed him again.

Then she said good-bye to the others of the cast who had shown up, including the austere Harrison Hobbs, who said, "Mind you don't get in any more trouble!"

"I'll be terribly careful. I hear New York has as much crime as London!"

Then she and Edward boarded the jet that would land them in New York within a few short hours. She could hardly believe it as the giant plane took off. She and her husband-to-be spent the time blissfully making plans and sleeping for a little. She tactfully avoided asking him what sort of message he had left with his mother.

Her father was at the New York airport to greet them. She thought he had never looked more healthy and happy. It was to be expected that he approved of Edward, and they became fast friends at once.

Then there was the excitement of the city, which, after London, her father solemnly assured her, was surely the greatest in the world. The marriage itself took place in a salon of their hotel the following day. Her father was there, and so were some of his friends from the Stratford company. Edward's guests at the wedding were from the cream of the New World society and from the top sporting circles. Vanessa noted that the press were present, and photos were taken that, by the magic of wireless, would be in the London newspapers in the next edition.

New York City was a wonderful place to honeymoon. They spent a lot of time at the theaters and often went backstage to visit with her father. Vanessa had never seen him so contented with his work and with life in general. And she herself had never known so much happiness.

Inevitably the few weeks they had in New York went

by. She considered herself lucky that she'd spent Christmas and New Year's with her one living parent. Now it was more than a week into the new year, and time for her and Edward to return to London. Return to Norville House. She knew that Edward's mother had sent him a long cable after the wedding had been reported in the London newspapers. And also that Edward and his mother had several long phone conversations. He merely told her that his mother was pleased, and Vanessa asked no other awkward questions. She was determined their honeymoon should not be spoiled.

Her father was at the airport to see them off to England again, and he made it a point to take her aside and say, "I shall return to England in a few months for the next season at Stratford. Even though you are now married, you always have me to turn to when you have problems. I want you to remember that."

"I will, Father," she said, kissing him warmly.

He gazed at her with some concern. "What about your stage career?"

"Edward and I will have to work that out," she said lamely.

"I hope you are able to," her father said, for the first time allowing his concern to be visible to her.

She and Edward boarded the jet, and she turned once to wave good-bye to her handsome British father. They found their seats, and she thought how wonderfully lucky she was. She had a father and husband who were full of love for her, and a future that should be without problems. There were no complications on which she and Edward couldn't find a meeting point. Nothing could harm their happiness. Not even the cold Lady Norville waiting to greet them in Blake Square. Nor the curse of the Brides of

Saturn, which she was sure they had overcome.

Her blond, good-looking husband glanced at her as the plane took off. "Frightened?"

"Never, when I'm with you," she said, taking his hand in hers.

"That's what I like to hear, my sweet Capricorn bride," he said with a laugh.

She smiled back. "I'm over that! I refuse to believe that silly old legend!"

"Excellent!" Edward said as they rose above the clouds on their way back to England.

Unhappily, their mutual bliss was to be short-lived. They were less than an hour out of New York, roaring ahead in the vast darkness, when an ominous message came over the plane's loudspeaker, "Because of an emergency situation, we shall be forced to land at Gander, Newfoundland. There is no need for undue alarm. But we must land at Gander!"

Vanessa heard the curt warning, and a stab of fear shot through her. She didn't dare turn to look at Edward. She knew that only a brief time ago they had defied the curse of the Brides of Saturn! Were they now to be punished for their defiance?

Chapter Six

As the great plane proceeded through the night, it occasionally was subject to moments of startling vibrations. The captain offered several messages of reassurance and informed them that the Newfoundland airport was not far distant. For the most part, the morale of the passengers was excellent. Perhaps because they felt nothing really serious could happen to this modern giant of the airlanes.

Vanessa and Edward continued to hold hands. There was a new meaning in the gesture now. Neither of them said anything, perhaps because they were afraid that voicing their thoughts might unleash suppressed fears surging within them. Vanessa wondered whether a centuries-old curse on the Norville family might now be endangering the more than one hundred lives of those on board the huge plane.

The captain spoke again, warning them that they were about to land in Gander and that the landing could be rough. Then they experienced the deafened ears and general tension common to such planes losing altitude. The jet seemed to be plunging down madly. But abruptly it came under control for a rocky journey down the airstrip and finally rolled to a halt. There were exclamations of relief among the passengers, and then a few cheers.

A fleet of buses conveyed them to a reasonably modern but shabby airport. It wasn't long after this that a message came over the loudspeaker telling them that another jet had already been dispatched from New York to land at Gander and take them on for the rest of the journey. The news was greeted with a muted enthusiasm by those who were already weary of waiting at the isolated airport.

Vanessa and Edward found empty stools at the coffee bar and had cups of black coffee, which made them feel a little better. Edward gave her a wry smile, and said, "You can't say we're not having every sort of experience."

"I know," she agreed. "I suppose this will be another big story for the newspapers."

"I wouldn't be surprised," he agreed. "Right now, I'm not worried about anything but getting on to London."

It was still pitch black and raining a drizzle when the other jet arrived. They were bused back to the big airliner and soon were in the sky again. Not too much later, the first signs of dawn appeared, and it was a bright, crisp January day when the plane finally set down in London.

They took a taxi to the city, and as they neared Norville House, Vanessa felt her nerves grow taut. She had no idea how she would be received by her awesome mother-in-law. Edward had also grown silent, and she judged that he was a little worried about the same thing.

At last the taxi made its way into Blake Square and pulled up before the gray majesty of Norville House. Almost at once the bald Norris came out to get their bags and greet them. He smiled and shook hands with Vanessa, offering her polite congratulations. Then Edward escorted her into the house. He halted at the door and made a gesture of picking her up and carrying her over the threshold. In spite of her tension, this made her laugh, and she was still laughing as he set her down on her feet to face her stern-looking mother-in-law.

Lady Norville gave her first attention to Edward. She rushed up to him and kissed him and then in dramatic fashion exclaimed, "You have no idea how worried I've been about you!"

Looking uncomfortable, Edward asked, "You heard about the plane trouble?"

"It's been on the wireless all day!" his mother said with a grimace. "I was sure the plane must have crashed, though they insisted it hadn't. They lie so!"

Edward tried to be cheery. "There wasn't a thing to be upset about, Mother. We just had a little delay while we waited for the second plane." He turned, and placing his arm around Vanessa, said, "And so I bring you home a new daughter!"

The coldness returned to his mother's manner as she said, "Yes, I know." And to Vanessa she said, "Welcome to Norville House! I have prepared your apartment as best I could." But she made no effort to kiss her.

Vanessa said, "Thank you, Lady Norville. I'll try not to be a nuisance."

The older woman ignored this and told her son, "There have been dozens of calls for you. Some of them important, I'm sure. Norris wrote them all down."

"I'll check them," Edward said. "But just now we'll go upstairs and freshen up a bit."

"You must be dreadfully tired," Lady Norville said to her son, without including Vanessa.

They made a quick retreat from the grim woman, hurrying up the winding stairway to the apartment on the second floor that they would occupy. Norris had already taken their luggage up. When they were safely in the apartment

107

with the door closed, Edward took her in his arms.

He kissed her and said, "You behaved magnificently under fire!"

She gave him a worried look. "She was so grim! I don't know whether I can manage it."

"Of course you can," he assured her heartily. "Mother will come around. I can see that. I know her better than you do, and I've seen her much worse than she was just now."

"I find that difficult to believe," she said.

"It's true," Edward insisted. "What you need now is a good sleep. You'll want to be rested for dinner."

"What about you?"

He glanced at his watch. "I'm afraid I can't afford the luxury. I'll have to go down and check those telephone calls and see what has been happening. But I'll be all right."

So he left her, and she began unpacking and then stretched out on the big bed and almost immediately fell into a deep sleep. She slept until she was wakened by a young girl in a maid's uniform standing in the bedroom doorway and timidly knocking on the open door.

"I'm sorry to disturb you, ma'am," the girl apologized. "Norris sent me up to help with the unpacking and to run your bath before dinner."

Only half-awake, she lifted herself up on an elbow. "Thank you," she said. "Is it getting late?"

"Yes, ma'am," the girl said. "Dinner will be served in an hour."

"Then I must hurry!" Vanessa said, and rose from the bed quickly.

The girl's name was Mary, and she had come over from Ireland to become a maid. She'd been working for the

Norville family for three years. She was talkative and a good worker. In no time she had the bags completely unpacked and everything put away. At the same time, she offered a good deal of gossip.

She informed Vanessa, "Mister Leonard is back living here now."

"Oh?" she said, as she sat before the dresser after her bath. "I thought he lived in Soho."

"He did for a while," the maid said. "But lately he's been doing better."

"I'm glad to hear it."

"He's had his hair cut shorter, and he's dressing more like a gentleman should," Mary confided. "And I understand he has a job of some sort."

"Good for Leonard," Vanessa said as she worked at her makeup. She wondered if the artistic young man might have decided that he was likely to inherit the title and estate and so had begun preparing himself for it.

"Lady Madeline Smith and he have been going places together," the maid went on. "She's the one who was once engaged to Mr. Edward."

Vanessa smiled at the girl. "My former rival."

Mary blushed. "No offense intended, ma'am. But I couldn't help mentioning it, since in the old days Lady Madeline did nothing but poke fun at Mr. Leonard. And now she seems pleased he's taking her out."

"Things do change," Vanessa said, rising. "Now, if you'll just zip me into my dress, I may manage to get down for dinner on time!"

When she entered the elegant living room with its soft lighting, she looked for her mother-in-law and saw she was not there. But Judge James Norville was standing by the big fireplace with a smile on his round, jovial face.

Glass in one hand, he came to greet her.

"My dear Vanessa," he said, kissing her. "How wonderful that you decided to marry Edward."

Blushing, she said, "It was all done in a bit of a rush."

"No harm in that!" the old man said. "Edward will be much happier with a wife, and you will do a lot to liven up things in this grim old house."

"Thank you," she said. "I've been hearing some interesting things about your son."

"Indeed," the judge said in a pleased tone. "Here he comes now, so you can tell him about it yourself."

She turned to see Leonard coming down the length of the big room toward her. There had been such a marked change in him, she barely recognized him. His hair was cut to a reasonable length, and he was wearing a tailored dark suit with vest and white shirt graced by a crimson cravat. He extended his hand to her and showed a look of goodwill on his thin but pleasantly intelligent face.

"Hello, Vanessa," he said. "I'm glad you went through with it. Edward is a lucky man!"

"Thank you," she said. "You're looking marvelous!"

Pride showed in Leonard's face. "Things have been breaking right for me."

Interested, she asked, "How?"

He said, "You know, I've always dabbled in art, and I have a special interest in scene design."

"You told me," she agreed.

"A few months ago I took some sketches to ITV for one of their television programs," Leonard said. "They liked what I had done and offered me a job on their stage-design staff. That is what I'm doing now!"

His father spoke up with parental delight, saying, "You should see some of his sets. He's creating some of the best

110

backgrounds on television.''

Vanessa gave Leonard a warm smile. ''I'm so happy for you. You're finally doing what you wanted.''

''I am,'' he agreed. ''And in a way, I owe it to you.''

''To me?'' she asked with surprise.

He nodded. ''I admired the way you fought to get a part in the West End. You told me about it that night we first met. And I realized I simply hadn't been trying hard enough.''

''You gave the lad inspiration,'' Judge Norville said. ''I told you I expected you to be an asset to the house.''

She smiled. ''I really don't think there's any credit due me, but I am delighted that you've made a place for yourself in a difficult field.''

''I'm doing special sets for a new production of *Peter Pan* that's being shown next month,'' he said. ''I've been working overtime. But I wasn't going to miss tonight.''

''That reminds me,'' Vanessa said. ''I wonder where Edward is? I haven't seen him since we arrived.''

Judge James Norville cleared his throat discreetly and said, ''I believe he's in the library with his mother at the moment. She had something to discuss with him.''

''I see,'' she said quietly. She had her own ideas of what the discussion might be about. No doubt Lady Norville was berating her son for his hasty marriage in America.

Leonard seemed to read her thoughts, for he gave her a smile of reassurance. ''I'm pouring myself a sherry,'' he said. ''I think you might do well with one.''

She nodded. ''Please. I'd like a sherry.''

Judge James Norville took advantage of his son's going to pour the drinks to tell her, ''You mustn't worry about Edward's mother. She's a very possessive person, and she

111

was bound not to turn Edward over to another, younger woman without some struggle.''

''I understand that,'' Vanessa said, ''but I'm also a little worried about something else.'' She raised her eyes significantly to the huge portrait of the first of the Brides of Saturn above the fireplace.

The stout man followed her glance and gazed at the fine oil painting of that early Lady Norville for a brief moment. Then he told her, ''I think you'd best forget all about that.''

''Will the rest of you do the same thing?'' she asked.

He showed embarrassment. ''I would hope so. I can't answer for Lady Norville, of course. But I'm sure that time will cure her objections to you as a daughter-in-law, even though you were born under the sign of Capricorn.''

Leonard returned and handed her a glass of sherry. He said, ''That's very good! From the ample Norville wine cellars. Have you visited them?''

She took the sherry and sipped it. ''It is good. I was only in the cellars for a moment when Edward gave me a general tour of the house.''

Leonard said, ''You'll have plenty of time to become acquainted with them now.'' His friendly manner of conversation was part of the marked change in him.

She said, ''Thank you for the encouraging note you sent me at the theater.''

His smile was shy. ''I felt I wanted to let you know that the family weren't all hostile to you.''

''You accomplished that very well,'' she told him.

The judge asked, ''Did they ever get that scoundrel who attacked you and robbed you in the theater alley?''

''No,'' she said. ''Not that I've heard of. Though they

may have done something on the case since I left England.''

"I don't think so," Leonard said. "I'm sure I would have heard or read something about it.''

"I'd like to have the villain in my court,'' Judge Norville stormed. "I'd see he received a sentence that would keep him off the streets for a while.''

The conversation was brought to an end by the arrival of Lady Norville, with Edward leading her in on his arm. There was a look of cold triumph on Lady Norville's patrician face, which Vanessa decided meant no good for her. After Edward had seen his mother safely to her chair, he went to get them drinks. When he passed Vanessa on his way to the sideboard, he apologized, "Sorry! Mother had a few problems for me.''

"I rather expected that,'' she said quietly.

He gave her a "you-know-how-it-is-with-Mother" look of appeal and went on to get the drinks. Meanwhile, Lady Norville took over the conversation with news of a successful fashion show conducted by herself and a group of friends. She did not omit to mention, "I think Lady Madeline Smith made a stunning model! She looked lovely in everything she wore.''

Leonard said, "She told me about some of the gowns. They sounded rather special.''

Edward, looking weary, took a stand beside Vanessa and in a lone voice told her, "I'm exhausted. There were a lot of business matters to be looked after. I finally realized I wouldn't have time to shave or change.''

"You're quite presentable,'' she said to him with a small smile.

"Good,'' he said with a sigh, and took some of his

drink. Then he told her, "Remember Hawkins?"

"The trainer who doped Flying Anne?"

"Yes. He's been seen around some of the sporting pubs in town again. I hope I can finally catch up with him."

"I think you should forget all about it. It's over," she worried.

"I'm afraid that's impossible," was her young husband's reply. "By the way, I had a message from Augustus Gordon. He's filming here in London, and he wants us to get together soon."

"I'd like that," she said.

"We'll have him here to dinner one night," Edward promised.

Lady Norville rose from her chair at that moment and led them all to the dining room. Again she conspicuously ignored Vanessa—and it seemed this was the way it was going to be.

Vanessa did not mind the first few weeks of being back in London. At Edward's suggestion she directed the redecoration of their apartment in the great gray mansion. This kept her busy for a while. She also went to see several plays, and Augustus Gordon had her out to the film set where he was working. He introduced her to the American director as a talent to be watched. She loved every minute of the experience.

On the way back in Augustus Gordon's limousine the star asked her, "When are you resuming your career?"

"I just don't know," she admitted.

"Have you discussed it with Edward?" the star asked.

"No. He's been so busy since we've arrived home."

The handsome Augustus looked quietly amused. "Getting ready for the new racing season?"

"That's part of it."

"Then he should be considerate of your wishes to begin acting once more," Augustus said. "My director is doing another film here in England. I think he might like to use you."

Her eyes widened with delight as she turned to the man seated beside her in the comfortable back seat of the limousine. "Honestly?"

"Yes."

Then regrets shadowed her face. "I daren't even think about it until I discuss it with Edward."

"Do it as soon as you can," the star said. "I'll be at Norville House for dinner next week. Try to have an answer for me by then."

"I will try," she said. "But I can't promise."

The handsome face of the star showed a hint of mockery as he went on to inquire, "How are you making out with Lady Norville?"

"We're managing. We don't see too much of each other. It's a large house."

"Has she forgiven you for being a Capricorn and allowing her son to marry you?"

"I hope so," she said. "I'm sure none of the others believe in that stupid old legend."

Augustus lifted his black eyebrows. "So now it is a stupid old legend. We have progressed! At one time you told me you were very worried about it."

She blushed. "I don't think you're very fair reminding me of that."

He reached over and patted her hand. "Sorry! I suppose I'm still piqued at Edward snatching you out from under my nose. I did want to marry you myself, remember?"

"I remember," she said, giving him a small smile. "And I look upon you as my dearest friend."

"Always do that," the star said, suddenly solemn.

He kissed her when he left her at the door of Norville House and again reminded her that he'd been invited to dinner the following Thursday. Vanessa was not liable to forget, since it would be her initial dinner party since arriving at the old mansion as Edward's wife.

At the last moment Edward suggested that they have an intimate dinner party in their apartment for Augustus rather than making it a family affair downstairs. Lady Norville was ill in her own apartment with a head cold, and neither the judge nor Leonard had planned to dine at home that night.

"Better we do this on our own," Edward suggested.

Vanessa was actually relieved at his decision. There was a dumbwaiter in the apartment on which all the food could be sent up piping hot, and Norris could be depended on to supervise the serving.

As they were dressing for dinner she mentioned for the first time the film role that Augustus Gordon had spoken about. She said, "Gus thinks he can get me in the next film. Would you object?"

Standing by her and tying his tie in the dresser mirror, Edward suddenly frowned. "Yes. I think so."

She glanced up over her shoulder at him. "Why?"

"I want you to give our marriage at least a year before you start acting again. Doing a play or a film is bound to take too much of your time."

"But I have time to spare!" she protested. "I have trouble getting through some days."

Edward gently touched her shoulder and in a pleading tone said, "You promised before we were married! Please keep your promise. If you go straight back to acting, it will only make things more difficult for Mother."

She gave him a resigned look. "Mother again!"

"I know what is best," he said with a hint of stubbornness that made her realize his mind was not to be changed for a while. He quickly donned his jacket and said, "What about the wine?"

"Norris didn't mention it. Probably he's chosen it."

Edward said, "I like to make my own choice. And you should learn something about it as well."

"Must I?"

"Yes," her husband said. "Just a moment ago you were complaining of not having enough to do. Now you're trying to escape a duty that is yours."

She put on her Capricorn necklace, which she rarely wore but which she thought went well with her black-velvet gown. She told him, "I'm wearing my necklace tonight. Your mother won't be on hand to be annoyed by it."

He smiled. "Why not?" Then he said, "We'll pick up a couple of flashlights in the kitchen, and I'll take you down to the wine cellar and show you our stock and how you go about making the proper choice. Tonight the main entrée is veal, isn't it?"

"Yes," she said. "Do I really have to go down to that musty old cellar? I'm all dressed!"

"I'll guide you, and it won't take more than ten minutes," Edward said. "Come along!"

Because she knew he'd made his mind up to it, she didn't argue any longer. One of the things that seemed to give him the greatest pleasure was showing her how to manage the big house. They picked up flashlights from Norris, who was in the kitchen seeing that dinner was being properly prepared. Edward told the very polite man-servant that they were going down to select the wine.

They each carried a flashlight, which they didn't use, since the cellar lights were working properly. Edward explained that the wiring in the dark underground cavern was ancient and not too dependable. As he guided her along in the deep-shadowed regions he said, "That's why I always bring a flashlight along."

They reached the area of the wine cellar that she recalled from that brief earlier tour of the old house. She remembered his mention of secret passages connecting Norville House to the other homes in the region of Blake Square and the legend that there was a hidden passage that joined with a maze of underground tunnels ranging throughout the city.

The dull yellow light bulbs spaced overhead at long intervals gave sufficient light to see the way. But there were many shadowed areas left. They reached the wooden door of the wine cellar, and Edward unlocked the padlock. Opening the heavy door, he showed her inside. There were at least two dozen racks for holding the wine bottles in a dozen or so tiers reaching from near the earthen floor to the beamed ceiling.

He showed her where the various vintages were kept and lifted out a dusty bottle occasionally to show her the name of the winery.

He said, "I think tonight we ought to use a good-vintage light red Burgundy."

They were busy selecting the vintage when Vanessa was suddenly aware of an apologetic Norris standing in the doorway of the wine cellar.

The bald manservant spoke in his clipped fashion, saying, "I'm sorry to disturb you, Mr. Edward, but there is a long-distance call for you."

"Blast!" Edward said, glancing up from the bottle he was holding. He turned to her and suggested, "You wait here a moment. I'll be right back. Familiarize yourself with some of the other wines."

Before she could make any sort of reply, he was hurrying off with Norris to answer the phone. She did not particularly like being left alone, even though the sparse overhead lights were sufficient to protect her from the darkness. She moved along the racks and occasionally selected a bottle from one of the many tiers, blew the dust off it, and read its label. She was busy doing this when without warning the cellar lights went out.

She stood there with the bottle in her hand, startled at being suddenly plunged into darkness. Edward had warned her the lighting system in the cellar was unreliable, and this was surely turning out to be the case. She stood there waiting for a moment, and then she remembered the flashlight she had and at once turned it on. Using its light, she replaced the bottle from the spot from which she'd taken it.

The darkness continued, and there was still no sign of Edward returning. Restless, she moved toward the door of the wine cellar, lighting her way with the beam of the flashlight. What she had in mind was going partway to meet Edward on his journey back to her. But when she left the wine cellar, she realized she didn't know the huge cellar all that well. She wasn't at all sure of being able to find her way.

Now she began to be more uneasy. She stood there in the grim darkness flashing the beam of the light around her. And she was suddenly aware of the distant sound of running water. Edward had suggested it might be from the sewers. The thought of the sewers suggested rats and all sorts of unpleasant things. She began to feel definitely nervous.

Fear sprouted quickly, and she worried why Edward was gone so long. In a mild panic she took a few steps forward and then halted because she knew she could be going in the wrong direction, actually walking away from where she might find Edward.

She was trembling a little, and she had a strong impulse to cry out Edward's name. She realized she'd made a mistake in not remaining in the wine cellar. Now she was wandering about in the black vastness of the main area, and it would be all too easy to lose herself or stumble into some sort of danger.

Thoughts of the legend and the ghosts that must surely inhabit the ancient mansion came to mind. She fought to keep calm and knew it was a losing struggle. She stood there on the edge of panic, rigid in her fright. Then suddenly from a distance and to the right she heard a low, gloating chuckle! It was such a malevolent sound, it sent her fears soaring!

Wheeling around, she shone the beam of her flashlight on the spot from which the chuckle had come. To her utter shock, the flashlight beam revealed the outline of a crouching figure in some sort of brown robe and cowl. Then the beam found the face of the crouching creature! She screamed as she saw the features of a gargoyle! A nose long and hooked over a twisted mouth, glittering insane eyes, and a long bony chin!

Vanessa stumbled back and screamed again. And as she did so, the ghostly creature vanished. Vanessa still continued to scream until she saw Edward's flashlight glowing in the darkness. He shouted to her in reply and came running toward her.

"Why are you so frightened?" he asked as he joined her.

She pointed to the spot in the shadows where the ghost had been. Brokenly she told him, "I've seen her! I've seen the ghost of the old witch!"

"What's this?" he said, turning to search the shadows with the beam of his own flashlight.

"She was standing right there! The witch of the legend! The one who put the curse on the Brides of Saturn!"

Edward's arm was around her trembling shoulders as he challenged her, "Now, wait a moment!"

"It's true!" she insisted, her teeth chattering.

"What happened to the lights?" he asked, almost angrily.

"I don't know," she said. "They went out almost as soon as you left me."

"Must be a faulty fuse," her young husband grumbled. "Why did you leave the wine cellar?"

"I thought I'd meet you partway."

"You should have stayed there," he said. "We'll pick up a bottle of wine and get back upstairs before you're in hysterics."

"I did see something!"

"We'll discuss it later," Edward said in a weary tone.

They found their way back to the wine cellar and he quickly selected a bottle. She waited at his side, feeling ashamed and aware that this lesson in wine selection had not been a success. Then they made their way toward the stairs.

At the stairway Edward found the switch controlling the

cellar lights. He pressed on it, and the lights came on. He looked around him in disgust. "What do you make of that? It looks as if someone accidently turned off the lights."

"How could they?"

He shrugged. "Don't ask me. Perhaps Norris did it without thinking. He's a great one for small economies about the house."

"I can't imagine his doing it, knowing I was still down here alone," she protested.

Edward said, "One of the other servants might have seen Norris and me come up, and assumed we had left the lights on by accident. Not knowing you were also down here, they put the lights out."

"Why couldn't the ghost have done it?" she demanded.

Edward gave her a shocked glance. "Don't say things like that! You look terribly upset, and we have company coming at any minute."

"I *am* terribly upset," she lamented as he helped her up the stairs.

"What will Gus think?" he worried.

"I don't care!"

They reached their apartment, and Norris was already there seeing that the table in the dining room was properly set and instructing the maid. Edward gave him the bottle to be served and asked that he see that Augustus Gordon was shown directly to their apartment. Norris politely observed that this was being looked after.

Edward then guided her into their bedroom and shut the door. Facing her, he demanded, "Now, what exactly did you see?"

Newport

Alive with pleasure!

Newport
20 CLASS A CIGARETTES

Newport

MENTHOL KINGS

mg. "tar," 1.2 mg. nicotine av. per cigarette, FTC Report April 1976.

Warning: The Surgeon General Has Determined That Cigarette Smoking Is Dangerous to Your Health.

"I saw a crouched figure in brown," she declared, and went on with the details.

Her young husband listened with a growing frown on his handsome face. When she ended her account, he said, "It sounds like the witch, all right. But I think I can tell you what it really was."

"What?"

"Your imagination!"

"Don't try to tell me that," she protested.

"You've heard those ghost stories, and when the lights went out, your nerves got the better of you!"

"Won't you give me credit for ordinary common sense?" she asked him pleadingly.

"You weren't harmed!"

"I might have been."

"But you weren't," he insisted. "I can't discuss it with you any more for the moment. Try to get it out of your mind."

She gave him a defiant look. "I can't forget it, and I won't deny it!"

Edward eyed her helplessly. "Now we're getting some of your Capricorn traits!"

Vanessa was groping for a reply when there was a polite knock on the door and Norris announced through the panel, "Your guest has arrived, sir."

"Thank you, Norris," Edward called out. To Vanessa he said, "Come along!"

"In a moment," she said unhappily. "You greet him first. I want to check my makeup again."

He left her to greet Augustus in the living room. She gazed at herself forlornly in the dresser mirror. She looked pale under her makeup. The fear still showed in her.

Quickly she applied some extra makeup, and then, summoning all her determination, went on out to join her husband and their guest.

Augustus Gordon was in a jovial mood. He greeted her warmly and kissed her. They stood around with drinks for a little, chatting about the various things that make up the small talk between friends getting together after an absence.

Augustus turned to her suddenly and said, "Are you taking good care of yourself?"

"I try," she said. "Why do you ask?"

The star smiled. "I think you look a little peaked. Forgive me, I was about to use that old cliché, you almost look as if you'd just seen a ghost!"

It hit her with full impact. She glanced across at Edward, and because he was standing there with his eyes imploring her not to give way, she managed a light, "Nothing like that! I've been rushing too much today. The strain of my first dinner party, you know."

Chapter Seven

Dinner went very well. Afterward they sat and talked, and Vanessa attempted to put the eerie incident in the cellar out of her mind. But she wasn't completely successful; it still remained there in the background of her thoughts, nagging her. Augustus Gordon was at his most entertaining, but she only half-listened to what he was saying.

At last the famous star got up from his easy chair and said, "I must be going. I can see that Vanessa is weary."

"Not really!" she protested, rising at the same time.

"Won't you have a good-night drink?" Edward asked his friend.

"I think not," Augustus Gordon said. "I have to be on the movie set early tomorrow morning." And he turned to her and asked, "Have you thought about that film part, Vanessa?"

She shook her head. "No. I'm afraid it's out of the question."

The star's eyebrows raised. "It could be a great opportunity for you."

Edward spoke up. "We both realize that, Gus. And we thank you. But I feel she needs her full time to get used to life here. She will have more social duties to take over as my mother relinquishes them."

The handsome actor eyed him wryly. "Sorry. I'd forgotten how the titled gentry live. You do have a full complement of chores, don't you? And special dispensations from the crown as well. It's a way of life quite foreign to a common chap like myself."

Vanessa saw her husband's face crimson and knew that Augustus Gordon had deliberately chosen his sarcastic words to annoy him. Trying to ease the situation between the two men who had been such longtime friends, she said quickly, "Don't blame it all on Edward. I agree with him fully in this. I want to make a success of being his wife before I do any more acting."

The star shrugged. "In that case, I can only say I hope you make your adjustments here quickly so that you may return to us."

They saw him to the door after his limousine had been called. When they had said their good nights to him, they returned to their apartment. Norris and his efficient staff had already cleared away all the dinner things.

Edward poured himself a stiff drink and flung himself down into the nearest easy chair as he exclaimed angrily, "I think Gus went a little too far tonight, even for a friend!"

She sat on the arm of her husband's chair. "You mustn't be too angry," she said. "He does believe in my ability, and he did want me to have that part in the film."

"He's interfering!"

"He doesn't see it that way."

"I'm afraid I do," Edward complained. "The fellow has a hate thing for the gentry."

"Because he'd like to be part of it. He's told me that himself."

"He has a lot to learn before he takes his place in proper

society," Edward said with disgust. "I hope we finally made the situation clear to him."

"I'm sure we did," she said quietly.

Edward looked up at her worriedly. "You weren't yourself all evening, and that made things more difficult. I glanced at you several times when Gus was talking, and you seemed miles away."

She got up and walked a few steps to the middle of the room before turning to face him. Reproachfully she said, "You are not allowing for the fright I had in the cellar."

"Sheer nerves! There was nothing important enough to brood about all evening."

"I saw the witch figure!"

Edward downed the rest of his drink. "I think we ought to go to bed. I don't want to discuss that again."

"You see?" she said with a kind of grim resignation.

This continued to be her husband's attitude in the days that followed. Worse than that, he seemed to have little time to give her. Plans for the operation of his stables in the coming season were taking more and more of his hours. As a result, she was left a good deal on her own.

Lady Madeline Smith appeared at the house for dinner several times as Leonard's guest. The friendship between the young scenic designer and the titled beauty seemed to be in full fruition. Lady Norville always welcomed the auburn-haired beauty and never missed an opportunity to have Vanessa show up badly when compared to the other girl.

Vanessa learned to expect this and accept it without a word. She did this for Edward, who she knew was as upset about it as she was. Lady Madeline Smith was so elated with her conquest of the reformed Leonard that she even deigned to be coolly friendly with Vanessa. But this did not put Vanessa off her guard. She knew Lady Madeline was her enemy.

Vanessa made it a point to avoid the cellar or any other isolated area of the house where she might find herself a witness to other supernatural happenings. She continued to be desperately afraid of the old house. Often she would go and stand below the large portrait of the first Lady Norville and worry about the legend. She thought about Madame Gina, the astrologer, and made up her mind to go there for a return visit one day. She knew the woman was a kind of charlatan, but she also had an idea the weird old gypsy was possessed of a general ability to gaze into the future and predict it.

Of course, she never dared mention her to Edward. One day she was in the living room gazing up at the portrait of that first doomed Capricorn bride when she heard a floorboard creak behind her and turned to see Leonard standing there.

He said, "You still have my lady ancestor on your mind?"

With a wry smile she said, "My behavior betrays me."

The young scenic artist studied the huge portrait with an interested eye. He said, "Whatever else she was, she was a beauty."

"She was," Vanessa agreed. "But I understand the legend has it that she lost her beauty later to a fearful plague."

Leonard gave her an amused smile. "That is part of the legend. You have kept it well in mind."

"Yes."

"I'd try to forget about it," was his advice.

"Edward says the same thing," she admitted. "But it is not all that easy."

"You've been married awhile, and nothing dreadful has happened thus far."

"We've had a few close calls," she pointed out. "Suppose we've just been lucky?"

He said, "Then think you are going to continue having the same good luck."

"I'll try," she said with a wan smile. No need to burden him about her meeting with the ghost in the cellar. Instead she asked him, "How are you making out at the television studios?"

"*Peter Pan* went well," he said. "I'm now working on another assignment. My problem is to get enough time. Madeline Smith wants me to attend a charity benefit with her tonight, and I should be working."

She said, "You need some change."

"I know, but I begrudge the lost hours," the new and more pleasant Leonard said.

She smiled. "Lady Madeline Smith seems to have changed her mind about you."

"I know," he said, amused.

"When she and Edward were courting, she rarely ever mentioned your name."

"Or spoke of me in a disgusted manner," the young man in the well-tailored dark suit was quick to admit. "Of course, I seemed a very different person to her then. A hippie from Soho had no appeal for her. You were the only one who saw that I had prospects. You were a kindred soul! I recognized that at once, and it gave me courage."

"I'm glad," she said.

"I'm not deceived about Madeline. She's shallow, and I accept that. She's company, and my going with her pleases my aunt."

"You couldn't delight Lady Norville more," Vanessa

said. "It helps make up for her disappointment that Edward married me."

"My aunt is stupid in that," Leonard declared. "Mother and Father think you're a fine addition to the family. And I needn't add that so do I!"

She smiled and touched his arm. "I was so pleased to come back and find a stalwart defender here in you. I expected you to still be doing the hippie thing in Soho."

"I was happy there," the young man said. "But when you've finished with it, you've finished with it. That is all behind me now."

"Will you marry Lady Madeline?"

"Never," he said.

"Better be careful. She may think you are serious."

"I've told her."

"Girls never believe what young men tell them," she warned him.

Leonard smiled. "You're probably right. I've been a little concerned with the situation myself. But it will take a little while to disengage myself gracefully."

"Lady Madeline can be overwhelming," she said. "She could make it difficult for you."

"I think I'll know how to handle it when the time comes," Leonard said. "If everything else fails, I can always tell her I'm reverting to being a hippie."

Vanessa laughed. "That would surely scare her off!"

One afternoon when she was alone in their own apartment, she had a phone call from Augustus Gordon. After a moment given over to the ordinary exchange of greetings, the star said, "I have some plans I'd like to talk to you about."

"Oh?" she said.

"Can you meet me within the half-hour?"

130

"I don't know." She hesitated.

"You know very well," he said somewhat acidly. "Are you or are you not busy?"

"I'm not busy," she said.

"Then meet me, and we'll have tea together," the famous actor said.

"You know I can't discuss any work contract," she warned him.

"I know that," Augustus Gordon replied wearily from the other end of the line. "The truth is, I'm lonesome for us to have one of our talks. And I need your advice."

"Very well," she said. "I don't expect Edward back until late. He's gone to see a horse at an out-of-town stable."

"Meet me at one hundred Thread Street," the star said. "It's a small street off Piccadilly Circus. Any cabdriver will find it. And I'm in the shop of John Fitzgibbons, wigmaker and theatrical costumer. It's a small building squeezed in between two larger ones, and he occupies the entire building."

She wrote down the address and told him, "I'll leave right away."

She did, and though it was snowing lightly, she was able to find a cab just outside Blake Square. She gave the cabby the address, and he headed toward the theatrical district.

It proved to be a short journey. She paid the taxi and got out in front of an ancient building with a murky-looking big window on the ground-floor level. In large letters in gold leaf across the window were the words "Fitzgibbon, Wigs and Costumes." A brown curtain on a brass rod mounted midway up the window shut off any view of what might be going on inside.

Vanessa opened the solid wood door and found herself in a huge, high-ceilinged room with stairs leading to a gallery at its rear. There was a long counter on the right as you entered, and in the display case of the counter were all sorts of wigs on stands. On forms at the back of the shop were costumes of a clown and a soldier of Victoria's day.

Augustus Gordon was standing near the back of the shop talking to a short, squat man with a florid face, spectacles, and a bald head with only a fringe of gray hair. The little man wore a kind of apron, and he eyed Vanessa with an interested smile as she entered.

The star came to her and kissed her on the lips. Then he took her down to the little man and said, "Lady Norville, this is John Fitzgibbon, the best and most honest wig-maker in all London!"

"I'm glad to meet you, Mr. Fitzgibbon," she said, amused at the star's emphasis on her title.

The little man smiled with delight. "Glad to meet you, your ladyship. Mr. Gordon claims you are the daughter of James Masters. He has often been in my shop."

"Nearly everyone in the theater business knows Father," she said.

Augustus Gordon took her by the arm and said, "I don't see you often enough to share you with John! So, come along!"

She laughed and said, "Good-bye, Mr. Fitzgibbon. I hope I may meet you again."

The little man waved a pudgy hand in farewell. "I have no doubt that you will, your ladyship."

When they were out on the street in the light snowfall, she gave the star a look of humorous reproach. "You didn't have to pile on that 'ladyship' business. You embarrassed me!"

Augustus pretended surprise. "I thought you'd be accustomed to it by now. As Edward's wife, you're entitled to be addressed in that fashion."

"I prefer to leave the honor with his mother," she said. "Where are you taking me for tea?"

"The nearest spot," he said. "It happens to be the Piccadilly Hotel."

So they soon found themselves seated in the somewhat shabby but pleasant old dining room of the famous hotel. A pianist played in the background as they faced each other across the table.

"What did you want to ask me about?" she said, curious.

The handsome actor smiled. "Nothing. I lied. I was anxious to spend an hour with you."

She shook her head. "A fine trick! I'll remember in future. Suppose I'd neglected something to come here."

"You told me you wouldn't be, before I allowed you to come," he reminded her as the tea things were served.

Over the cakes and hot tea, she asked, "What are your plans?"

"A new play pretty soon," he said. "How are you making out at Norville House?"

"Fair," she said.

The actor asked bluntly, "Does Lady Norville still hate you?"

She didn't know whether to be amused or indignant. She finally said, "Isn't that an ugly question?"

"I only ask it because I'm worried about you. I didn't think you looked too happy the other night when I had dinner with you."

"Oh, that," she said.

He nodded. "I think Edward is blind to the hostility

toward you in that old house.''

"Maybe he has to be. He hopes that gradually his mother will feel differently about me.''

"I wouldn't want to bet on it,'' Augustus Gordon said grimly. "What about his uncle, the judge?''

"The judge is kind to me. And his wife, Edith, is at least civil. She doesn't avoid me as Edward's mother still does.''

"That needn't mean she's your friend. People of her class can be extremely discreet.''

"I know. But she is happier since Leonard has found a career for himself.''

"Leonard is Edward's cousin?''

"Yes. He's changed completely. Become serious about his work as a scenic artist and is nice with me. He's dating Edward's old girlfriend, Lady Madeline, at the moment.''

Augustus Gordon listened to this with a knowing expression on his handsome face. "You realize that Leonard would probably get the title in the event anything happened to Edward. He's probably grooming himself just in case the legend of the Brides of Saturn come true again.''

"Edward and I don't talk about the curse anymore.''

"You think about it. I can tell it by the strained look in your face.''

Vanessa was upset. "You don't mean that!''

"I do,'' the famous actor said gravely. "Why were you so troubled the night I dined at Norville House?''

She hesitated, then decided she might as well tell him. She had no one else in whom she could confide. It would be eight weeks or more before her father came back from his tour in America.

She said, "I had a fright just before you came.''

"A fright?"

"Yes. We were in the cellar choosing wine. Edward had to leave me. When I was there alone, the lights went out and I saw something."

Augustus Gordon was listening intently. "You saw what?"

"A figure in brown. A creature with a horrible face. It looked like a witch."

"The witch of the legend," he said with meaning.

"I don't know," she said unhappily. "Edward thinks I conjured the figure out of the shadows with my imagination."

"What do you think?" the man across the table from her asked tautly.

She hesitated again. "I saw something."

He stared at her and sat back in his chair. "I don't like it! I don't like it at all!"

"I'm not sure about it," she said nervously. "I don't think we should make a lot of it!"

"When is your father due home?"

"Probably it will be two months."

"Too long," the actor said with a frown. "I wish he were here now to advise you. I think he'd tell you your marriage was a mistake!"

"Oh, no!" she protested.

"Listen to me," the handsome star begged her. "There is too much going against you. Too many people in that old house who hate you!"

"I love Edward!"

"And you're merely a pretty possession to him," Augustus Gordon said bitterly. "He doesn't appreciate your talent or want you to do anything with it. He wants you there in that great old house wilting away from the hate around you. And all the while he's busy with his stables!''

"That's not completely fair," she protested.

Augustus Gordon's hypnotic eyes met hers. "It is far closer to the truth than you dare admit. Edward took you from me, so I can be completely honest. I think that sooner or later the marriage will break up, and it would be better for you if it broke up at once.''

"No!" she said.

He gave a deep sigh. "I've told you what I believe. Think it over. I'll say no more. But in the end, I predict you'll say I'm right and you will leave Edward. That is, if nothing awful happens to either of you in the meanwhile. You are a Capricorn, and he braved the curse to marry you."

Vanessa said, "And because I'm a Capricorn, I'll see this through. We're not weaklings! It's a strong star, and I mean to live up to my birthright."

In a gentler tone the star said, "I hope that it does work out well, for your sake. But I doubt it."

When they left the hotel he suddenly consulted his watch and said, "I've stayed with you longer than I intended. I'm due to meet my agent at this very minute."

She hurried to say, "Don't worry about me getting home. I'll find a cab. And anyway, it's stopped snowing."

"I'll find you a cab, at least," he said, moving forward to try to flag down a passing one.

"Don't!" she protested. "I want to stroll a little in the air. You go on to your agent's. His office is near here, isn't it?"

"About five minutes' walk in the opposite direction from the one you're taking," a worried Augustus said.

"You're sure you don't mind if I leave you?"

"Not at all."

"Very well, then," he said. "I'll phone you from the apartment later and make sure you arrived home safely."

"I'll manage very well," she said. "Don't forget, I'm used to being in London on my own."

He smiled and kissed her. "Take care, and think about what I had to say."

And then he left her. She stood there for a moment and watched his tall, impressive figure vanish among the crowds in the theater section. She thought ruefully to herself that it wasn't likely she'd forget their discussion. It had been much more frank and brutal than she'd expected from him. He didn't think she had any future at Norville House at all. This made her wonder if perhaps he might be right.

She started walking along the familiar streets she had traveled every day when she'd been acting in the Augustus Gordon company. She was in a depressed state of mind, which the bleak late afternoon did little to dispel. She made her way, lost in the dismal thoughts that the actor's words had brought to her, and hardly knew where she was. Suddenly she saw a familiar sign ahead of her.

It was the black-and-white sign of Madame Gina, astrologer and fortune-teller. Remembrance came flooding back to her of her visit to the massively fat old gypsy that other afternoon. She recalled every detail of the strange experience, and while she knew the old gypsy probably preyed on trouble, she still had the odd conviction that Madame Gina had true powers of prediction.

The fact that she was here before the doorway leading to the fortune-teller's quarters seemed to have some special significance. She stood there on the narrow, busy sidewalk debating whether she should go up and consult the woman again or not. There were many things she wished she knew about the future. If only Madame Gina could give her a single true prediction, it would be worth the time.

A shiver went through her. It came partly from the cold of the street and partly from her own despair. Dusk was fast settling, and if she went up to visit the fortune-teller, it would be dark before she arrived back at Norville House. But she knew Edward was going to be late. No harm would be done if she were not home for an hour. She debated it all with herself for a few seconds more and then turned and began the ascent of the dark stairs.

The hall was very dark at the third-floor landing. She hesitated in the shadows before the door with the sign on it. Then she knocked on the door and waited. But no one came. She stood there in the pungent atmosphere of decay that the old hallway exuded and wondered whether the old gypsy might be out somewhere. Because of her massive size, it did not seem likely that she left her apartment often.

Feeling somewhat more tense, Vanessa knocked on the door again. And again there was only silence. She stood there, aware of a strange sensation of fear that was quickly surging through her. It came to such a peak that she could not remain there any longer. Turning, she began a frantic descent of the narrow, rickety stairs, stumbling on the way. At last she reached the street.

The fear she had known was still with her, but to a less intense degree. It was almost dark, and she saw a sickly light in the shop of the cobbler's on the ground floor of the ancient building. Something impelled her to go to the dusty-glass-paned door of the cobbler's shop and open it. She went in and saw an elderly man on a stool, busy placing a heel on a shoe. Hammer in hand and nails in his mouth, he glanced at her.

He slipped the nails from between his lips and paused in his work to ask, "What is it, miss?" a bored expression on his thin, beard-stubbled face.

She couldn't find the words for a moment. Then she said awkwardly, "Madame Gina? I went up to see her. No one answered my knock."

The old man deserted his bench and got up and came over nearer her. He said, "No one answered?"

"No."

"That's odd!"

She nodded. "I wondered if she might have left without taking down her sign."

The cobbler shook his gray head. "She didn't leave. Not her!"

"Would she be out somewhere, then?"

"No. There's a lad does her errands for her." The cobbler squinted at Vanessa in the murky light of the single dusty bulb overhead. "You say you've seen her?"

"Yes."

"Then you know what she's like. Weighs a bloomin' ton! She ain't been down or up them stairs since she moved in. Then I thought she'd never make it gettin' up there!"

Vanessa began to feel that she'd made a fool of herself. It really wasn't important to her. She said, "I'm sorry I bothered you about it. It was just that she didn't answer the door, and I thought you might know the reason why."

"I don't."

"She's probably sleeping, or maybe she doesn't want to give any readings," Vanessa suggested.

"She'd want to give readings," the cobbler said with

139

emphasis. "She likes the money! Not that she's all that good at parting with any of it. I have a hard time getting my rent."

"You're the landlord?"

"I look after the building for the owner," the cobbler said with a hint of pride. "You're not the first one to come in here today and tell me they couldn't get any answer up there."

"Oh?" she said, not knowing what to say.

"You're the third, as a matter of fact," the old man said sharply, rubbing his grizzled chin at the same time.

All Vanessa wanted to do now was make a retreat. As quick a retreat as she could. She said, "Perhaps she is ill."

The cobbler's thin face took on a new expression of interest. "Maybe she is!"

"Could you phone her?"

"I have no phone."

"That is a problem," she said.

"But I do have a key," the old cobbler said. "And I think I ought to go up there and find out what is wrong."

Vanessa was quick to say, "There may not be anything wrong!"

"Just the same, I think I should have a look," the old man said, obviously concerned now that he'd given his mind to the matter.

Vanessa moved toward the street door. "I hope it's nothing serious."

"Just a minute!" the cobbler called after her, to keep her from leaving.

Hand on the door, she nervously said, "Yes?"

"I want you to go up there with me."

She gasped. "Why?"

"I want a witness."

Unhappily she said, "I'd like to, but I'm in a hurry. I really can't take the time."

The cobbler gave her an annoyed look. "Why not? You said it might be important! That she might be sick!"

Panic swept through her as an inner voice warned her that she had somehow gotten herself involved in something dreadful. She felt as she thought a drowning person must feel after stupidly toppling into the water. She had plunged herself into this situation by her own blundering!

She said, "There's nothing I can do. You will soon know whether or not she's ill."

"Matter of principle," the old man said, coming close to her, a strange gleam in his eyes. "I don't intend to go up there without a witness with me. No telling what I'll find, or what she might say I done up there!"

She listened to his argument, which was so meaningful to him and which she was not at all interested in. And yet she knew that she had insinuated herself into this sleazy world and was now an actor in the little drama taking place there.

In a desperate last-ditch struggle to get away, she said, "I'd be a hindrance rather than a help! I'm terribly nervous!"

The cobbler asked, "Who says there'll be anything to be nervous about? She's probably in her bed sleeping after having a pint or two. Likes her beer, she does!"

Feeling as if she were hypnotized, she found herself on the street with the little old man as he carefully padlocked his shop after him. Then he took her by the arm and led her to the doorway and the stairs beyond it. She mounted the stairs with a growing feeling of dread.

"I think perhaps we shouldn't disturb her," she said despairingly.

141

Panting from the exhaustion of making his way up the stairs so quickly, the old man said, ' Too late to think about that now!''

Vanessa was on the verge of nausea. Her panic continued growing as they ascended the last flight of stairs. And when they reached the dark, dank hallway before the door of Madame Gina's place, she leaned against the wall weakly. The old man had a good deal of trouble with the lock, and grumbled in a low voice to himself. She felt dreadfully afraid of it all and debated whether she might successfully bolt down the stairs to freedom as he busied himself with the lock.

But she waited too long. With a triumphant exclamation, he turned the key, and the door opened to his hand. ''There we are,'' he said. And to her, ''Come along! You'll do no good as a witness staying out there.''

Miserably she followed him into the hall of the tiny apartment. She knew that just beyond, in the dusk, there was the larger room with the crystal ball on the table. This was where the massive old gypsy had made her predictions earlier.

The cobbler was a few steps ahead of her, and suddenly he halted and gasped. Then he turned to her and gave her a signal to join him. Biting her lower lip, she slowly covered the short distance, sure that she was on the verge of some horrible discovery and not wanting to know what it might be.

''Look!'' the cobbler pointed.

It was now so near dark that she couldn't make out any of the details. But she did see the massive body sprawled on the floor by the table. The chair in which she'd been sitting was overturned, and the crystal ball in which she'd seen her visions of the future lay shattered on the floor beyond her outstretched hand.

In the macabre moment Vanessa found herself wondering whether the fat old woman might not have had a last glimpse into the future before she collapsed. A vision of her own death!

In a taut voice she asked, "Is she dead?"

"Don't know," the old cobbler said. "Look away, if you like. I'm going to turn on the light."

"Thanks," she said, her stomach heaving as she leaned again on the nearest wall.

The old man turned the single bulb on in the room where Madame Gina lay. She heard him move over to the body and mutter to himself. He was there only a moment or so. She waited with her eyes averted from the grisly scene.

The cobbler came back with a grim look on his wizened face. "She's dead, all right! Been dead some time! She's cold to touch!"

"I'm not surprised," she said weakly.

"Why?" the old man wanted to know.

She tried to find a reason. Tried to explain that somehow she had known from the very first moment when she'd stood before the door that Madame Gina was dead. But she was sure he wouldn't understand. So she murmured, "There's the smell of death in here!"

"You think so?" the old man said uneasily. "It was her heart. All that fat and all that beer! I warned her! Now she's gone!"

"Yes," Vanessa said in a low voice. "Now I'll go."

"Not yet!" the old man said sharply. "You can't leave yet. You're my witness! You got to wait until the police get here!"

"The police?" she asked dully.

"Yes," the old cobbler said. "I'll use Madame Gina's

143

phone to get them!'' And he left her to go to wherever the phone was.

Vanessa leaned weakly against the wall of the hallway near the door to the room where the woman's dead body lay. She was too upset to think clearly. She didn't dare move or turn her head. She could not bear to look upon Madame Gina in death. And she cursed herself for ever having the impulse to come up to the fortune-teller's apartment again.

Why?

And then a new feeling of horror came to her. Perhaps she had been sent here to receive a message. A message that even now Madame Gina was able to offer her. The old gypsy had warned her of future dangers before. Perhaps now her mute, cold body was giving another message. A message of death!

Chapter Eight

The police finally arrived. There were three of them, a plainclothes inspector and two police officers. They quickly took in the situation and questioned the cobbler and Vanessa. It was all strictly routine, as the stout Madame Gina had apparently died of heart failure.

The inspector told Vanessa, "You can leave now, Lady Norville. It's not likely we'll have to bother you about this again."

She was still in a confused and depressed state. Her murmured "thank you" was said in a low tone.

The middle-aged inspector gave her a concerned glance. "Are you all right, Lady Norville?"

She touched a hand to her temple and managed, "Yes. Quite all right. It has been a bit of a strain. I was anxious to leave, but the landlord felt I should stay."

The inspector glanced inside the apartment, where the cobbler was still giving information to one of the policemen. Then he turned back to her. "It's too bad you stumbled into this. I'd try to forget all about it if I were you."

"I will," she said.

"I'll see you safely into a cab," the inspector told her. And he accompanied her down the narrow stairs to the street. It was dark and cold. He stepped out to the curb and hailed the first passing taxi and helped her into it. She had a last glimpse of his concerned face in the open doorway of the taxi as he said, "I'd stay away from these gypsy fortune-telling places if I were you, my lady."

"I intend to," she assured him.

He shut the door and then gave the driver her address in Blake Square. Vanessa sat back against the taxi seat and shut her eyes as it made its way through the busy streets. She was still shattered by her experience. More than anything else she wanted to get home and see her husband.

Edward had arrived at Norville House first. He was impatiently waiting for her in the apartment when she came in. He rushed to meet her with his handsome face troubled.

"Where were you?" he asked. "You left no message. I came home earlier than I expected, and you weren't here!"

She crumpled in his arms and burst into tears. Edward at once tried to comfort her, and when her first wave of despair was at an end, he gently questioned her. He led her over to the divan and sat with her as she told him about her eerie adventure.

Edward heard her out and then asked, "Why should the death of this woman bother you so? You'd met her only once before."

She shook her head. "It's hard to explain. It was like some sort of evil omen. That's what it seemed like to me. I was caught up in it, and I couldn't escape!"

"I think that police inspector gave you excellent advice when he told you to keep away from gypsy fortune-tellers. You know such places aren't safe."

"I've learned a lesson," she said.

"I hope so," Edward told her. "Had the woman been alive, you might have found yourself in worse trouble. She would have at least taken more money from you for her fake predictions, and you might have been robbed as well!"

"It's over! I just want to erase it from my mind if I can!"

"You must!" her young husband said. "I blame Augustus for a good deal of this. If he hadn't lured you downtown to meet him, you wouldn't have gotten into this trouble."

"You can't blame him! He had nothing to do with my going to Madame Gina's place."

"But he had you meet him to try to talk you into some sort of acting job again. I know him!"

"Please!" she protested. "It only makes things worse to have you angry with Augustus."

Edward said, "I'm not going to quarrel with him. But we've made plans to go out together on Wednesday night, and I'm going to tell him then that I don't like his keeping at you about the theater."

Vanessa said nothing to this. She knew Edward could be stubborn about such things, and she didn't want to make a bad situation worse. For the moment her life returned to a normal routine, and the nightmare of finding the dead gypsy woman faded from her mind.

She remembered that Edward and Augustus had planned a night on the town like the ones of their bachelor days. Because she hoped it would help strengthen the friendship between the two, she was happy about the arrangement. It meant her having dinner with Lady Norville and the others alone, but it was something that she'd steeled herself to face.

What she hadn't expected was Lady Madeline Smith as a dinner guest. When Vanessa went down to join her mother-in-law, the judge, and Leonard, she found Lady Madeline standing there with them, looking every inch the upper-class beauty.

Leonard hurried to pour Vanessa her usual cocktail as Lady Madeline gave her a mocking smile and said, "I hear Edward is out on the town tonight! Fancy his deserting you like this so soon after your marriage!"

Vanessa felt her cheeks burn. "I encouraged him to go out. He and Augustus are having dinner at Edward's club and then moving on to a few drinking places they like."

Lady Madeline arched her perfect eyebrows as she exclaimed, "How droll!"

Lady Norville spoke up from her chair, saying, "Augustus and my son were friends long before Edward met Vanessa. In fact, it was through Augustus that Edward did get to know her."

"I remember very well," Lady Madeline said with a taunting smile for Vanessa. "She was doing that little part in that rather poor play."

Judge James Norville coughed and said, "I thought the play was jolly good! And the night I saw Vanessa in it, she received a round of applause on her exit."

"Really?" Lady Madeline said dryly, as if it didn't matter at all.

Leonard came back with Vanessa's drink, and his face showed a flushed, uneasy expression. He said, "I know Augustus felt Vanessa had a great future in the theater, and he hasn't forgiven Edward for marrying her and taking her away from show business."

Lady Norville gave him one of her cold looks. "You theater people think your world is the only one. I suggest

148

that we talk about something more important! I understand we may soon be having newer and higher estate taxes. What have you heard about this, James?''

''It's by no means certain,'' the stout judge said in his pompous manner. And he went on to discuss the tax problem at an interminable length.

Vanessa sat quietly with her drink and felt grateful to the old man for his long-winded addition to the conversation. She thought that he was doing it mostly to help take the attention from her. Lady Madeline Smith threw herself in a nearby chair and scowled at her drink as the monotonous monologue went on. Her bear-baiting of Vanessa was over for the moment. Leonard managed to give Vanessa an encouraging wink and a small smile by standing behind Lady Madeline's chair, where his effort at communication could not be seen.

Eventually they went in to dinner. As soon as possible afterward, Vanessa excused herself and went up to the apartment to read. She sat reading by the fireplace in the apartment living room until it was eleven. Then she put her book down and went to the window to glance out at Blake Square. It was a dark night, and it had begun to rain.

She felt that Edward should soon be home, and began to worry a little. As time passed and he still did not arrive back, her tension increased. By midnight she was pacing the floor. And when one o'clock came, she was thoroughly upset. She debated rousing Leonard and asking his aid in helping find her missing husband, and then she discarded this idea on the grounds that he might have gone out somewhere with Lady Madeline.

Instead she decided to try reaching Augustus at his apartment. In fact, Edward might even be there. And if neither of them were at the apartment, they would still be out somewhere in one of the many pubs they'd planned to visit.

She went to the phone in the living room of her apartment and called the number of Augustus Gordon's apartment. And to her utter surprise, the star answered the phone himself. She asked him about Edward.

Augustus sounded surprised. "Isn't he home?"

"No."

"I left him an hour and a half ago," the star said.

Her concern grew. "Then he should be here by now!"

"I know."

"What do you think?" she said, trying to disguise the panic that had crept into her voice.

"I wonder," the star said. "At one of the pubs a fellow came up and told Edward where he might locate Hawkins."

"Hawkins?"

"Yes. The fellow who was his horse trainer. The one who skipped after doping Flying Anne."

"I remember," she said worriedly.

"Edward was quite excited about the information," Augustus went on. "I told him to forget it. But he said he intended to look up Hawkins and settle with him."

Fear in her voice, she asked, "Do you think he may have gone after him tonight?"

"It's a possibility," the star admitted. "Come to think of it, he was edgy all the rest of the evening. As if he had something on his mind. He couldn't wait to be rid of me."

"Do you remember the address or anything else the man told him about Hawkins?"

"No. They didn't want me to hear. The fellow took him aside. But Edward was so full of it, he told me afterward. But no details."

150

"I don't know what to do!" she said despairingly.

"Wait a little," the actor told her. "I'm sure he'll show up. Edward knows how to take care of himself."

"Gus, I'm really worried!"

"Take it easy, darling," the star consoled her. "Pour yourself a drink."

"He may have headed straight into danger!"

"I think not," Augustus said. "But he may be wasting time trying to follow up what is probably a false lead. If he doesn't get back in an hour, phone me again."

"I don't want to keep bothering you!"

"I'll want to know," Augustus said. "I'm as upset as you are. But I have faith in Edward being able to take care of any tricky situation."

She gave a deep sigh. "I hope you're right. I'll let you know when he arrives."

"Do that!" the actor said. "And don't forget to pour yourself that drink. Best thing for the nerves!"

Because she was desperate, she followed his advice. She found a bottle of brandy and poured a good, strong drink in a snifter. But she did not feel like drinking. She had to force herself to sip it as she sat with her eyes fixed on the face of the clock on the wall opposite her. As the minute hand neared two o'clock, she jumped up from her chair in a frantic state.

Fear was taking over. She rushed to the phone and this time called Leonard's number in the suite he occupied in the old mansion. Never had the place seemed so oppressive. The old fears revived to augment her fresh ones. Was the curse at work again?

She let the phone ring until Leonard answered it, sounding surprisingly awake for the late hour. She apologized for calling him at the late hour and said, "I have a problem. Edward isn't back yet!''

Leonard said, ''He's really having a night on the town! I just returned from squiring Lady Madeline, and I thought I was late enough! He and Gus must have found themselves some interesting company!''

''Gus isn't with him,'' she said unhappily. ''I've talked to Gus at his apartment. I talked to him more than an hour ago.''

''Then what's keeping Edward?''

''That's why I'm frantic,'' she said. And she went on to tell Edward's cousin what Gus had told her about Edward being given the address of the errant trainer. And of his desire to try to find him.

Leonard sounded skeptical. ''I can't think Edward would go on that sort of wild-goose chase at this hour of the night!''

''He has to be somewhere!''

''I know,'' Leonard said with a sigh. ''Are you up and dressed now?''

''Yes. I've been pacing up and down the living room. I'm almost out of my mind with worry.''

''Stop that!'' the young man at the other end of the line ordered her. ''I'll be up there in a moment.''

He was as good as his word. He came into the living room and at once asked her the same questions as on the phone all over again. The one good thing this did was occupy her for a little. But when he finished, she found herself on the edge of hysteria once again.

She could tell that Leonard was as worried as she was, even though he tried not to show it. He tried to divert her by talking of other things as they kept the long vigil for Edward.

Leonard smiled grimly. ''What a minx that Lady

Madeline is! I noticed the way she unsheathed her claws on you at dinner time.''

''Thanks to your father, she had to shut up,'' Vanessa said.

''Father knew what was going on, and of course he didn't approve,'' Leonard said. ''His experience on the bench stood him in good stead. He rambled on with enough mumbo-jumbo to confuse and sedate everyone, including Madeline!''

He had barely finished speaking when there was a knock on the door. Vanessa and he exchanged uneasy glances. She felt her throat tighten, and she rushed to the door and opened it. Norris was standing there in his dressing gown with a shocked look on his sallow face.

''What is it, Norris?'' she asked.

His eyes moved uneasily from her to Leonard standing behind her. He seemed relieved to see that Leonard was there and addressed himself to the young man. ''I think you had better come down, Mr. Leonard. The police are at the door.''

''The police!'' she cried. ''Is it about Sir Edward?''

Leonard pushed by her and said, ''Let me look after this, Vanessa.''

She followed him, and as he started down the stairs she grasped the arm of the upset Norris and demanded, ''Tell me what is wrong.''

The expression on the face of Norris told her there was something terribly wrong. She shook his arm and cried, ''Tell me, Norris! What has happened to my husband?''

Norris stammered, ''Really, your ladyship, I think one of the family should . . . I don't . . . It's not proper that . . .

Tears were streaming down her cheeks. ''Norris, what

has happened to Edward?''

Pain showed in the manservant's face, he gave a frantic look down the stairs, but there was no sign of Leonard coming back. He gazed at her with despair in his eyes as he said, ''The police found Sir Edward in the square. He's been stabbed!''

She felt a numbing grief as she questioned him dully. ''He's dead, isn't he?''

''I'm so sorry, your ladyship!'' Norris said in a stricken voice.

It was at this point that she collapsed. And when she came to in the apartment a little later, the nightmare continued. Leonard was with her, and so were the judge and Lady Norville. But it was the judge's wife, Edith, who had taken over the situation. She was moving about giving orders, and when she saw that Vanessa had come to, she rushed over and sat on the bed by her.

Edith consoled her. ''You mustn't try to think of anything for the moment. A doctor is on his way. Everything that can be done is being done.''

''Edward?'' she said brokenly. ''What about Edward?''

''The police are looking for his attacker and the weapon,'' the older woman said, sympathy showing on her lined face.

In a dry, lost voice, she said, ''Then he is dead?''

''Yes,'' Edith Norville said. ''You must be brave!''

It was the beginning of a time of extreme torture. She buried her face in her pillow and sobbed as she had never sobbed before. In time the doctor came and gave her some kind of strong drug. She slept, and when she awakened, she was given other drugs to calm her and carry her through the ordeal.

The happenings that followed were only vaguely remembered by her. There were the visits by the police, the arrival of Augustus, looking old and so sad, and the mourning of the others in the family. Edward's mother suffered a mild heart attack and had to be confined to her bed.

Fog returned the day of the funeral. Drugged to the hilt, Vanessa attended the service and went on to the graveside leaning heavily on Leonard's arm. The young scenic designer had been her chief source of comfort through all the moments of pain.

Then they returned to the house. Augustus bade her an awkward farewell, promising to call her soon. It was Leonard and his mother and father who accompanied her up to the apartment and remained to offer her the small comfort they could.

Judge James Norville suggested, "It might perhaps be wise for you to move to another section of the house. There are tragic memories here for you."

Seated stiffly in the high-backed chair, Vanessa, calm in her drugged state, told the old man, "No. I prefer to remain here. This was where Edward and I knew the most happiness."

Edith Norville showed a look of understanding on her matronly face. "Then stay here, by all means. You're only a moment away from the rest of us. It is not as though you were alone in a big house."

The judge nodded solemnly. "You may depend on us to do all we can for you."

"Thank you," she said. "You've done a great deal, as it is."

Edith said, "No more than we should." She turned to her husband and added, "I think you and I should go down and stay with Edward's mother for a little. She will want to hear about the funeral.''

''True,'' the judge said. And to Leonard he suggested, ''You remain here with Vanessa for a little.''

''I'm planning to stay as long as she wants me,'' Leonard said.

His parents went on downstairs, leaving Vanessa and the young man alone. She gazed up at him with gratitude in her lovely eyes. ''Thank you. You've been so good to me. Edward would approve so.''

Leonard sighed. ''I wish I could do more. But the pain is something I can't do anything about.''

''I feel so alone,'' she said. ''And until now, I never minded being alone.''

''You will get over this,'' the young man standing before her said earnestly. ''You've too much character to let this crush you. When you are ready, you should return to the stage.''

''As soon as I can,'' she agreed.

''Edward's mother will oppose it,'' Leonard warned her. ''But you must expect that and be prepared to fight for your own way of life.''

''I mean to,'' she said. ''For Edward's sake, I gave in to her too much. That is changed now.''

''As soon as you feel well enough, you might begin training classes to refresh you, something of that sort,'' Leonard went on. ''And then, within a few months you could take on film work or even return to the stage.''

''I mean to,'' she said. ''Augustus will help.''

Leonard gave her a knowing glance. ''He's bound to.'' And then he went on to say, ''You know, Augustus Gordon is in love with you still. I'd almost be willing to guarantee he'll ask you to marry him after a suitable interval.''

"I don't want to think of such things.''

"Sorry. That was heartless of me. I meant well and made a bad job of it,'' Leonard said awkwardly. "What I was trying to point out was that you have a guaranteed future with someone who really cares for you. If you want it.''

She frowned slightly. "I'm still in shock. And numbed with drugs. But now that Edward is gone, I'm not sure what my feelings are for Gus.''

"Plenty of time to decide.''

"I want to see whoever killed Edward punished, whether it be that Hawkins or someone else,'' she said. "That is what I care about most.''

"The police haven't come up with anything yet. But I feel they will.''

"They must!''

Leonard walked over and helped himself to a drink from a bottle on the sideboard. Then he slowly strolled back to her.

He said, "This grim old mansion was never meant for you. I felt that from the first.''

She raised her eyes to the young man, and in a taut voice she said, "Do you know what Lady Norville told me when I went in to see her after her heart attack?''

"No. She's capable of saying anything!'' Leonard said with disgust.

"She stared up at me and whispered, 'You killed him! You caused my son's death!!''' Vanessa paused. "What do you think? Am I guilty? I mean, because of the curse?''

Leonard looked upset. "I thought we'd given up belief in the curse long ago!"

"You're not answering my question."

"Of course you're not to blame," the young man said. "All that nonsense about a curse on Capricorn brides belongs back in the Middle Ages."

"If the curse is active, I will be the next to die," she said, too calmly. "And if I thought I were guilty, I'd want to die, and quickly!"

"You must stop that talk! And that sort of thinking!"

"I had an omen of this," she said. "I somehow knew that it was going to happen. I knew it, and I wouldn't face it. There was an old gypsy woman, and she died. And I knew! I just knew!"

Leonard came and placed a comforting hand on her shoulder. "You mustn't give way to morbid thinking," he told her. "Edward wouldn't want that."

"I know," she said.

"Did the doctor give you something to help you sleep?" the young man asked.

"Yes."

"Then take the sedative and go to bed. You badly need a good night's sleep."

"I realize that," she agreed. "The place is so empty without Edward."

"I understand," Leonard said. "That is why you mustn't allow yourself to mope alone here. It's not your nature to do it."

She rose from her chair with a wan smile on her pale face. "Thank you, Leonard. You've been a great help."

"I want to continue to be, if you'll allow it."

"Won't Lady Madeline have something to say about that?"

He frowned. "I'm not worried about her. She's been much too harsh in her attitude toward you. And I don't admire her for it."

"She was terribly jealous when Edward left her for me."

Leonard said, "She's really never forgiven you. At least she had the good taste to remain in the background at the funeral."

"I didn't see her."

"That was best," he said. "Had she come to you to offer sympathy, she'd have wound up saying the wrong thing."

"I don't want her sympathy," Vanessa said. "Nor do I want to be an object of sympathy here!"

"Don't worry about it," Leonard said. "Get yourself a good sleep. Then things will seem easier to face." He bent and gave her a brotherly kiss on the cheek.

She saw him to the door, and when she returned to the grim quiet of the apartment, her loneliness came back to haunt her again. She followed the young man's advice and took two sleeping tablets before she went to bed. As a result, she fell into a deep, dreamless sleep almost at once, and did not wake until the maid came with her breakfast the following morning.

She had ordered only orange juice, toast, and coffee, and she had difficulty managing one piece of toast. In addition to everything else, she had awakened with a strong feeling of nausea. And when she tried to leave her bed and take a shower, she collapsed on the way to the bathroom door.

Fortunately the maid was still in the apartment and at once summoned Norris. The dedicated manservant was the only one available, as all the others with the exception of Lady Norville were somewhere out of the house. And Lady Norville was still confined to her bed. With his usual good judgment Norris contacted the family doctor at a not-too-distant hospital and explained the situation. The doctor promised to come by and see Vanessa as soon as he completed his visits to his hospital patients.

Norris returned to Vanessa's bedside to give her this information, saying, "The doctor should be here within the hour."

Vanessa was distressed. "But I'm not that ill!"

"You were on the floor in a faint when I was called up here," Norris reminded her.

"I've been under a strain, and I felt ill," she said. "But not ill enough for a doctor."

Norris looked grave. "I think we ought to allow the doctor to decide that, your ladyship."

She gave a deep sigh. "I suppose if you've been in touch with him, there's nothing to be done about stopping him now."

"No, your ladyship," Norris said in his calm, polite fashion. "Should I inform Lady Norville of your illness?"

"Please don't!" Vanessa begged him. "She's not well herself. I don't want her bothered with my slight indisposition."

They left her alone for a little, and she lay back against the pillows and considered her plight. There was no doubt in her mind that the ordeal of losing Edward had resulted in her fainting spell. But she vaguely recalled having felt slightly ill on several other mornings. Being nauseated before breakfast was something new to her. Perhaps Norris was right. It was the right course to discuss her problem with a doctor.

Dr. Henry Mosher arrived a few minutes before twelve. He was a serious gray-haired man of medium build who had been the Norvilles' family doctor for some years. Now he came to her bedside with a questioning look on his long, lined face.

"What have you been up to this morning?" he asked.

She told him, ending with, "I don't think it's anything more than that I've been under great tension."

The doctor was showing new interest. He said, "Let me give you a brief examination," which he proceeded to do.

When he had finished, she said, "I know this is making a fuss about nothing."

His eyes met hers. "I wouldn't be too sure of that, Lady Norville."

"What do you mean?"

The gray-haired Dr. Mosher said, "I'll be blunt, Lady Norville, because I think this should be good news for you. I think you are pregnant."

"Pregnant!" she gasped.

He nodded. "Yes, I would say you are probably in your second month. We'll quickly make some tests. And if they prove positive, it should be the best of news for you. Sir Edward will have a son or daughter, after all."

The news completely stunned her. After the doctor left, she paced up and down the living room in her excitement. She didn't dare mention it to anyone until she was certain, and she had asked Dr. Mosher to keep the information confidential until after he informed her whether his diagnosis was correct or not.

But still she felt she had to talk about it with somebody. Not anyone in the family, and she had few close women friends. It was not surprising that the person she finally decided to speak with was Augustus Gordon. The star had always been close to both her and Edward. It was fitting she should turn to him.

Fortunately she was able to reach him at his apartment. She told him what the doctor had said and then in a tear-choked voice said, "If only Edward had lived!"

From the other end of the line Augustus said, "But you should be happy. If this is true, he is alive, in a sense."

"I had to talk to someone!"

"I'm glad you chose to call me," the actor said. "In fact, I'm flattered. When will you know with certainty?"

"The doctor hopes to be able to tell me tomorrow," she said.

"Then we will keep our fingers crossed," he said.

"I've been taking so many sedatives and sleeping tablets since Edward was murdered," she lamented. "I think I should stop until I know."

"What did the doctor say?"

"He didn't tell me anything about that."

Augustus said, "You can always call his office."

"I will," she said.

"How are you feeling generally?" he wanted to know.

"As well as I could expect."

"I want to see you soon," he said. "We have so many things to talk about."

"I know."

"How are things at Norville House? Is Lady Norville any better?"

"I think she is gradually improving. I haven't tried to see her too often. She's still in bed."

"This news should cheer her."

Vanessa sighed. "I don't want to count on that. She seems to hate me! It's been worse since Edward's death."

Augustus predicted, "I still say this will change her

attitude. You will be producing an heir to the title, if the doctor is correct. That is important in titled families and should be important to her as a mother, in any case.''

''I'll talk with her when I'm certain,'' she said.

''And don't forget to call me back again,'' Augustus warned her. ''Don't leave me dangling in suspense.''

She spent the rest of the day quietly. In the late afternoon she put through a call to Dr. Mosher's office and managed to speak with him personally. He told her it would be safe to continue taking the tranquilizers and sedatives he had ordered. He also promised he would call her the next day with definite word.

Vanessa had talked with her father by transatlantic phone the day after Edward was murdered. He had done his best to comfort her, and promised to return to England within a few weeks. Now she wished she could phone him again and tell him of this latest development. But better to wait until she was certain.

She worried what attitude the elderly Lady Norville would take. Knowing her mother-in-law as she did, she would not be surprised if the ailing woman set up a lament about bringing the child of a Capricorn Norville mother into the world. The legend seemed to weigh heavily on the older woman's mind.

Vanessa found it difficult to sort out her own feelings. She would dearly love to have Edward's child. But at the same time, she did not want to doom an unborn child to the violence of the curse. Edward's murder had caused her to do new thinking about the legend of the Brides of Saturn. And though she might not want to admit it, even to herself, she had come to fear the Norville curse.

She was still taking many of her meals in her own part of the old mansion. And she was debating about going down

163

to dinner when the phone rang. She answered it, and it was Dr. Mosher.

The doctor sounded excited, "I thought I ought to call you at once. I hurried the tests through, and I'm happy to be able to tell you that you are definitely pregnant."

She gasped. Then she said, "Thank you, doctor. I think it has to be the best news I've had."

"I agree," the doctor said. "And I'll be around tomorrow to talk to you and make sure you take care of yourself properly."

Vanessa put the phone down with a trembling hand. Edward was to live after all! Be reborn in her baby! She couldn't wait to tell the others. For the moment her joy in the discovery outweighed all the concern she'd felt about having such a child.

She rushed downstairs to the living room, where the members of the family usually gathered before dinner. Bursting into the elegant big room, she found Edith and her husband standing there. Leonard was standing over by the fireplace, and seated in the easy chair by him was none other than Lady Norville. The old woman looked grimly taut as she sat there with her hands cupped on the silver head of her black cane. Seeing Vanessa, the older Lady Norville glared at her.

Vanessa went straight to her. Kneeling by her chair, she said, "How good to have you up and around again!"

Her mother-in-law drew back slightly, as if with distaste, as she said stiffly, "It is the first time, and I may have to return to my room in a moment or two."

Vanessa's face was bright with her new happiness as she said, "I have some news for you first! Wonderful news!"

The old woman's lined features continued to reflect

164

hatred as she said with harsh scorn, "Wonderful news! What wonderful news could you possibly have for me?"

"I'm going to have a baby," she said simply. "Edward's child will be born in about seven months."

Lady Norville's eyes widened, and she exclaimed, "Edward's child?"

"Yes!"

The old woman shook her head and in a trembling voice told her, "No child of yours will take the place of my son! The son you condemned!"

Chapter Nine

Tears sprang into Vanessa's eyes.

At once the living room resounded with congratulations. The stout judge sputtered forth his good wishes, and even the usually quiet Edith cried out her joy at the news. Leonard came over and gently assisted Vanessa to her feet and turned her a little away from the old woman in the chair.

"You mustn't mind," he said. "It is the best of news!"

From the chair the elderly Lady Norville spoke up peevishly, addressing herself to the judge. "James! I feel unwell! Help me back to bed!"

The stout judge hurried to obey her, and the supposed invalid rose from the chair without obvious difficulty. She leaned on his arm as he guided her out of the room, but Vanessa was left with the feeling that her mother-in-law was not as infirm as she pretended. Her remaining in her own apartment was more an expression of her grief and anger than anything else.

The matronly Edith Norville came over to Vanessa and said, "You mustn't mind Edward's mother! She was so fond of him. And she is still in shock from the word of his death."

"Not to mention that she has always been a difficult person anyway," Leonard said.

Vanessa said, "I hoped she would be pleased."

"Any normal person would have been," Leonard said with annoyance.

"You mustn't judge too quickly," Edith Norville said. "I'm sure that my sister-in-law will realize how wrong she has been, and apologize to Vanessa later."

Vanessa worried, "I have driven her away from having dinner with all of you."

"No, I don't think so," Edith Norville said. "This is the first time she has appeared. I hardly think she planned to remain for dinner."

Leonard's intelligent face showed doubt. "I don't think she's all that sick. A lot of it is pretense."

His mother gave him a reproving glance. "She has lost her son! I know if anything like that happened to you, I would feel equally badly."

"Would you take it out on an innocent like Vanessa?" he wanted to know.

Edith Norville's face shadowed. She looked up at the great painting of the first Lady Norville still dominating the big room from over the fireplace. "Lady Norville has always believed in the legend. The curse of the Saturn Brides has been something in which she's believed. And she cannot forget that Vanessa married Edward even though she was a Capricorn!"

"That's idiotic nonsense!" Leonard exclaimed. "Edward was killed by thieves. Violence such as his murder is all too commonplace these days."

His mother gave him a meaningful look. "Be that as it may, your aunt thinks that Vanessa caused Edward's death by defying the curse. And she likely believes that Vanessa will die in the same way. She must believe it, if she accepts the curse."

168

"Even on those terms, Vanessa has put her life on the line. Marrying Edward was a courageous act, not a selfish one, as my aunt tries to make it," Leonard protested.

"Please don't argue about it," Vanessa said unhappily, all joy in her announcement vanished.

At that moment, Judge James Norville came back into the big room to join them. He said, "There's no need for concern. I have seen her safely into the hands of her companion. She is returning to bed."

Edith Norville asked him, "Do you think we should call the doctor?"

"No," the judge said. "She is not that unwell." Then he crossed to Vanessa, brushing Leonard aside, and solemnly told her, "You have all our good wishes. I'm sure you know that. It is a fine thing that Edward will have an heir."

"I wonder," she said. "Lady Norville doesn't seem to think so."

"She will when she has time to think it over," the judge assured her. "This will be a beneficial change in the will. There need be no recourse to my late brother's sealed instructions, as in the case of Edward's death without issue."

Vanessa realized for the first time that the birth of a child would eliminate any chance Leonard might have of falling heir to the title. Even Judge Norville might himself have been named next in line in that sealed envelope.

She said, "I'm sorry to come between you and the title."

"Not at all!" the judge protested. "We want to see the original line carried on. And this is the answer. I'm sure neither Leonard nor I am interested in titles."

Leonard said, "Vanessa knows that!"

169

Edith Norville smiled ruefully. "I shouldn't want to be another Lady Norville. The house wouldn't be large enough for all of us."

Vanessa remained downstairs for dinner. The three Norvilles were kind and tried to put her at ease. But she found herself unable to relax. The earlier scene with Lady Norville had been a shattering one. And now she sensed a certain strained atmosphere as she sat with the others. They were trying to overcome it, but not succeeding.

She thought of the many changes that had occurred since she had come to live at Blake Square. And she wondered if this gradual process of change mightn't be leading her to an accounting with the phantom of Norville House, just as it had happened with those other Brides of Saturn. Was she also doomed to die, as her mother-in-law had suggested? She tried to smother the fears that were tormenting her, without much success.

As soon as she could, she excused herself from the others. It was not until she was alone in her apartment that she really began to be afraid. In a desperate effort to fight her rising terror, she went to the phone and tried Augustus Gordon's number. The phone rang several times before he answered.

"It's Vanessa again," she told him nervously. "I was afraid I mightn't catch you in."

"You almost didn't," he said. "I was out to the River Club for dinner. I opened the door just as the phone began to ring."

"Thank goodness!"

"You sound upset."

"I am," she said. "It hasn't been an easy evening. But first let me tell you. Dr. Mosher called earlier than I expected. He says I'm going to have a baby. I'm two months pregnant.''

There was a brief moment of silence from the other end of the line; then Augustus said, "Good! I know this is what you wanted.''

"I think it is,'' she said. "But I'm terribly confused.''

"You're bound to be,'' the star said.

"What do you think?''

He said, "I think it will delay your return to the theater. I deplore that. But then, you couldn't begin acting right away in any case out of consideration of Edward's memory.''

"That's true,'' she agreed.

"So maybe this is the best thing for you. I'm sure the Norvilles will also be of two minds. It gives you a different position in the family. The mother of the heir.''

"I know,'' she said. "Lady Norville is still bitter. And Leonard and his parents are trying to be enthusiastic about it, but it does end any hope of their branch of the family inheriting the title.''

"I warned you about that,'' Augustus said.

She paused. "I'm frightened, Gus,'' she said, a shudder rushing through her. "I feel so alone!''

"You must call on that Capricorn determination,'' he told her.

"I hope I have it.''

"You have,'' he assured her. "If you're not happy at Norville House, why don't you leave it? Rent a flat somewhere. Find some friend to live with you. That Brady girl, the daughter of the wardrobe mistress, for instance.''

The prospect was too overwhelming. "No, I can't do that,'' she said. "The Norvilles would hate me for it!''

"It seems they hate you anyway," the star said dryly.

"Only Edward's mother."

"That would be enough to make me leave," Augustus Gordon said. "Look, I'll find you a flat. You needn't worry about anything. Let me get you a place."

"Thanks, Gus, I'll have to stay here," she said. "I feel it is what Edward would want."

"I see," he said with a sigh.

"Gus, do you think they'll ever solve his murder?"

"They usually do."

"But days have passed."

"It takes time."

"If the curse was responsible, it could take forever," she said unhappily. "Edward's mother thinks that is what brought about his death. She told me so again tonight."

"You promised you wouldn't listen to such things."

"I try not to," she said.

"Let us meet for lunch tomorrow and celebrate the baby," the star said.

"I'd like that. If you really want to."

"Of course I want to. Let's meet at the Dorchester. Say around one?"

"Fine!"

"I have to be at the BBC for a recording in the morning," he said. "But I'll meet you at the hotel. I'll be waiting in the lobby."

"Thank you, Gus," she said. "And forgive me for bothering you so much."

"What else are friends for?" he asked. "Go to bed early and try to forget everything but the baby."

Vanessa followed his instructions. Dr. Mosher had told her it was all right to continue taking the sleeping pills for at least a while. By ten o'clock she was in bed with the lights turned out. Whenever she glanced at Edward's side of the bed, a painful longing surged through her. Would she ever adjust to being alone?

Before her marriage, she had been content to live alone in her apartment and depend on those in the outside world for companionship. But now that she had known a happy marriage, she ached for the small joys of casual conversation and the intimate presence of someone loving and loved. Being by herself was as hurtful as an open wound, and made her wonder if she would ever be able to adjust to it. Of course she would! She must tell herself that!

Edward's baby would help. But slowly she must learn to be a separate person again, dependent on herself, able to live as she had lived before. Getting back onstage could be her salvation. She could not deny what the theater meant to her. When her father returned, they would talk about it. And maybe the bond between her and her parent would become stronger than it had been before.

She fell asleep with these thoughts in mind. How long she slept, she did not know. The sleeping pills always blurred her mind. But tonight they did not contain her in sleep. She opened her eyes to the blackness of the bedroom, and almost at once a sense of terror swept through her. Her thoughts were confused by the sleeping tablet, but she at once knew she was somehow being threatened.

She tried to waken herself to more alertness, without any success. The feeling of terror continued to grow, and she was sure she was no longer alone in the room. She heard the door from the apartment's living room creak open, and then, outlined in the doorway she saw the phantom figure she had seen that night in the cellar. The figure of the legendary Norville witch in brown robe with a shawl over her head!

The soft night-light in the living room neatly outlined the crouched figure. The ghostly creature hesitated in the doorway for a little and then began slowly to advance toward her.

"No!" she screamed, scrambling out of bed and standing drunkenly, her head reeling from the strong sleeping pills and her vision blurring and clearing alternately.

The witch gave no hint of hearing her terrified cry and came slowly across the room toward her. Now she could see its weird, ugly features. The long nose and the twisted mouth. Thin, bony fingers outstretched to grasp her!

"Help!" she cried, and stumbled to one side as the thing from the darkness lunged at her.

Her awkward movement saved her from the phantom's clawlike hands. And now she ran from the bedroom to the living room and the corridor beyond. She felt that once she made an escape to the corridor she would be able to rouse some of the others. It was her only hope of safety.

But the witch was in pursuit of her. She heard the quick footsteps coming behind her. With another scream she reached the door and flung it open, to race out into the dark corridor.

"Help!" she cried again.

She hesitated despairingly for a moment and then made for the stairway. Leonard's room was almost directly below. If she could only waken him, he would come to her rescue. But the phantom was behind her. And as she reached the head of the stairs, she felt the bony hands reach out and shove her hard down the broad stwirway.

She screamed again and reached out in a vain effort to break her fall. But it was useless. She plunged downward and blacked out.

Norris was close to her and worriedly saying, "Your

174

ladyship! Can you hear me, your ladyship!"

Vanessa wearily opened her eyes and saw the solemn face of the bald manservant looming in the soft light above her. She moaned and gasped, "The stairs!"

"You fell down all the way," Norris said. "I found you stretched out here!"

She looked around to see where she might be, and saw she was on the landing below. And the thought slowly formed in her mind that it was fortunate for her that both the stairs and the landing had a covering of heavy carpet.

"Are you hurt, your ladyship?" Norris asked.

"I don't know," she said quite truthfully. "Give me a moment."

Norris knelt by her in patient silence while she tried to straighten out her confused thoughts and discover whether she was seriously hurt. She had no obvious pain, but that could be because her senses were dulled by the sleeping tablets.

"What's happening?" This question came from a distance away, and it was Leonard's voice.

Norris turned and said, "Mr. Leonard, her ladyship has had an accident."

"An accident?" Leonard repeated, hurrying forward and also kneeling by her.

Vanessa gazed up at him. "I called for you. I tried to reach you."

Leonard said, "Let me get you back in bed. Do you think anything is broken?"

"I think not," she said.

"Very well," the young man said grimly. "You can follow us, Norris. I'll probably need you." And with that he swept Vanessa up in his arms and started up the stairs with her.

Still in a kind of daze, she found herself thinking that he was much stronger than she had ever given him credit for. He was one of those thin young men whose appearance was deceptive.

He placed her gently on her bed and asked again, ''How are you?''

''All right, I think,'' she said, knowing that it was a stupid reply but not able to make her mind work. Norris stood respectfully at the foot of the bed, as dignified in his dressing gown as in his regular clothes.

Leonard told the manservant, ''Get us a couple of brandies, Norris.'' And then he turned to her. ''I'd better phone the doctor, hadn't I?''

''No!'' she protested. ''I'm sure I'm not hurt that badly!''

Leonard gave her a knowing look. ''You have someone else besides yourself to think of.''

She hesitated. ''I'll talk to the doctor in the morning. It is so early in my pregnancy. I don't think I need worry.''

''What made you stumble down the stairs?'' he asked.

She found it difficult to explain with the lights on and him there. She said unhappily, ''I woke up and saw the witch! The legendary witch!''

Leonard's pleasant face showed embarrassment. ''You mean you had a bad dream.''

Vanessa sat up on an elbow. ''It was no dream! I saw the door open, and she was standing in the doorway. A horrible face and bony hands!''

''How do you know it wasn't a kind of nightmare?''

''It was too real!''

''Go on,'' he said, doubt in his voice.

''The phantom came at me! Then I somehow eluded her and made my way out of the apartment. I wanted to try to rouse you. I was calling out your name when the ghost came up behind me and shoved me down the stairs.''

Leonard stared at her without saying anything. Then he asked, "Don't you think you had a bad dream and tried to call me? That somehow you stumbled and plunged down the stairway?"

"No!"

Norris came with their brandies. Leonard gave her one, and took a sip from his own glass. Then he said, "We agreed not to believe in the curse."

She looked at him over the brandy snifter she was holding. "In this house it is difficult not to believe in it."

"You mustn't listen to the others. Don't lose the independence you had when you first arrived here," he said.

Norris coughed politely from the foot of the bed, and when Leonard turned to him he said, "Will there be anything else, sir?"

"No, I think not," Leonard said. "Better go back to bed."

"Thank you, sir," Norris said. And he bowed to her and added, "I trust your ladyship's injuries were minor."

"I'm certain they were," she said. "Good night, Norris."

The manservant left them, and Leonard remained seated on the side of her bed for a little. Then he finally asked, "Do you feel well enough to be left alone now?"

"Yes," she said. "I'll leave the light on my bedside stand on. That will make it better."

"Good idea," he agreed. "Don't let your nerves rule you."

"I'll try not to," Vanessa said, and a shadow crossed her lovely face as she went on with, "I wish you wouldn't mention what happened to the others."

177

"No?" He stood staring at her with mild amazement.

"It's better that you shouldn't," she said. "They wouldn't believe my story anyway, and it would only serve to reinforce Lady Norville's belief that the curse is working."

"That is a good point," the young man said. "As far as I'm concerned, I'm willing to believe you. But I hope you were mistaken. I'm not so good at battling ghosts."

"No one is," she said quietly.

He left her, and she kept the light on. It was now very late, and she knew she should seek sleep again. But sleep was elusive on this eerie night. She still saw the ugly face of the ghost in her imagination, still felt the touch of those cold, bony hands. Nothing would change her mind about what she'd seen. No matter how much Leonard or anyone else might rationalize, she knew she had seen the witch!

The strategy of having the light on worked better than she'd expected. In spite of her fears, she eventually fell asleep, and when she got up the following morning, she was in much better spirits than she'd been the previous night. In fact, all that had happened now had a nightmarish quality for her.

After the maid left her breakfast, she put through a call to Dr. Mosher. Leonard insisted that she do this. She could not reach the doctor at once and so left her name and address.

Now came the period of truly difficult waiting. She wanted to leave the old mansion but was afraid to go before she talked with the doctor. So she showered and dressed and waited nervously until at last her phone rang. It was Dr. Mosher.

She told him she had stumbled down the stairs. No need to have him doubt her sanity by mentioning the ghost. She

178

ended with, "I feel all right. So I don't think I was hurt."

"No one can know that better than you," the doctor said from the other end of the line. "But you must be more careful. Later on, a fall like that might result in your losing the child."

"I know that. And it is why I was worried," she said.

"How are your nerves?" the doctor asked, giving her a bit of a surprise.

"Not good," she answered. "I still have a certain number of sleeping tablets and tranquilizers. I'm taking them as you suggested."

"I'll work out a new program for you shortly," the doctor promised. "And do take care!"

She put down the phone with a wry face. It was almost comic advice he'd given her, in view of the facts. But she had not been able to tell him the facts, and never would be able to. She found her pocketbook and quickly made her way down the stairs.

Edith Norville was standing in the lower hall and gave her a questioning glance as she came down to join her. "Are you going out somewhere?" Leonard's mother asked.

"Yes," Vanessa said. "I have a luncheon engagement." She was independent enough not to wish to reveal whom she was meeting for lunch.

The matronly Edith said, "Do enjoy yourself. You deserve an outing."

Vanessa asked, "How is Lady Norville this morning?"

"I'd say there is very little wrong with her," Edith Norville said with a hint of disgust. "She is moving around her own apartment as nimble as you'd like. I sometimes wonder if that heart attack of hers wasn't shammed."

Vanessa said, "Edward's murder was a grim shock for her."

"For us all," the older woman said. "It has been a horrible business. I'm inclined to think she's made the worst of it rather than the best."

"I won't be too late getting back," Vanessa promised as she left.

She took a taxi and reached the Dorchester before Augustus Gordon. While she was standing in the busy lobby of the famous hotel waiting for him, she saw a familiar figure across the room. The man she saw also recognized her and came straight across to her. He was the inspector who had questioned her when Edward's lifeless body had been found behind a clump of bushes in Blake Square.

The inspector removed his pepper-and-salt hat and with a solicitous expression on his round face said, "Inspector Halliday, your ladyship. Do you remember me?"

"Yes, I do," she said. "I knew you the moment I saw you."

He smiled slightly in an embarrassed way. "You were under a great strain when we last met. People have a way of forgetting us."

"Not I," she said. "Is there anything new on the case?"

The inspector wrinkled his brow slightly. "Not that I know of, Lady Norville. Of course, these cases are never closed. You realize that."

"Are they usually solved? That is what concerns me."

"The Yard does reasonably well," the inspector said. "And a murder in Blake Square is far from an ordinary occurrence. It is an interesting area, that. Houses old, and all about the same vintage."

"Yes."

The inspector asked her, "Have you ever heard about there being passages between the houses, with one of them joining onto the underground sewage tunnels that run under all the old city?"

She said, "Yes. I have heard of them. As a matter of fact, it was my late husband who told me they existed. Though he claimed he had never been able to find them."

"Interesting," the inspector said. "We had a theory about the murderer. We think he may have come up into the square from some such tunnel and then vanished the same way. It would have cut down his risk of being discovered."

"Did you find the main tunnel?"

"Yes," the inspector said. "That wasn't hard at all. It connects with a passage to the Smith house. But we weren't able to find any such passage joining onto the cellar at Norville House, so that left us up against a blank wall. Still, one could be there. You might talk with Lady Norville when she is feeling better. We couldn't question her much at the time of the murder, she was so unwell."

"I will," Vanessa promised.

The inspector said, "If you find out anything, you might just call me at the Yard."

"Inspector Halliday, isn't it?" she said, going over the name to be certain she had it right.

"Exactly, your ladyship," the inspector said, and with a bow left her and donned his hat. She watched as he went on out of the front entrance of the Dorchester.

She wondered a moment what he had been doing there. But then there was no great mystery about his being in the hotel lobby. Members of the CID were called on to go everywhere. What had caught her interest was his mention of the secret passages and the fact that they had traced a connection between the main tunnel and a passage leading to the cellars of the house of Lady Madeline Smith.

She had not thought of Lady Madeline in connection with the murder. But she now began to wonder whether she had missed an important lead. Could Lady Madeline and Edward have had a secret meeting and a quarrel? And might not Lady Madeline have stabbed him and then fled by the secret passage? No one in her father's house would have seen her leave or return, and barring someone seeing her at the scene of the crime, she would be safe.

The idea haunted Vanessa. She was lost in a maze of her troubled thoughts when Augustus Gordon suddenly appeared and came up to her.

"You look as if your thoughts were miles distant," he said.

She managed a small smile for him. "I'm afraid they were."

"I'm sorry to be late," the actor said. "Blame the BBC. But I have a reservation, so there should be no delay."

There wasn't. The headwaiter had an excellent table saved for them, and Augustus and she enjoyed their meal. Over coffee she told him of her strange adventure of the previous night.

The star's black eyebrows raised in concern, and he said, "I think you must get out of that house. I told you so last night, and it is even more important now."

"No, I can't," she said. "Not yet."

He gave her a meaningful glance. "You might stay too long!"

"Now you're hinting about the curse," she said.

"I should think a Capricorn like you would sum up the

situation and make a fast decision.''

''I have a certain allegiance due the family and to Edward's memory,'' she replied. ''I think Edward's child should be born in Norville House.''

The handsome actor showed impatience. ''You're a romantic! An idealist! But then, those are also Capricorn traits. I might have expected them in you!''

''I'm sorry, Gus. I must stay on.''

''Even if you are murdered?''

''That is a chance I will have to take,'' she said. ''Besides, I now have some new leads to follow up.''

The star gave her a warning look. ''Leave the investigating to the police.''

''I mean to. But sometimes members of the family can help them.''

''Not you,'' he said. ''I'd say you were in enough trouble as it is.''

She smiled in a troubled fashion. ''Poor Gus! I have done nothing but upset you!''

''I think you would have been a lot better off if you had married me rather than Edward,'' was his reply.

''I'm sorry.''

''So am I,'' he said with grim resignation. ''I'm opening a new play, and I hoped you could at least understudy the leading lady. In that way, your name wouldn't be in the limelight. But now you have this child coming, and you can't even take on the role of understudy.''

''I appreciate your thought just the same,'' she said.

He gave her a sharp look. ''Do you really want the child?''

''I do,'' she said, so firmly that there could be no more discussion along those lines.

Gus saw her safely to a taxi, and they made plans to

meet again another day. In spite of the luncheon accomplishing nothing, it had at least cheered her up. And as she sat back in the taxi heading toward Blake Square, she realized it had also brought her in contact with the friendly Inspector Halliday again. And he had brought up the subject of the secret passages, which she'd forgotten about.

It was a natural consequence of the meeting that when she returned to Norville House her curiosity should still be aroused. And so she quietly armed herself with a flashlight and made her way down to the great cellar, being careful that no one saw her along the way.

The dank, dark cellar had always been an awesome place for her, and it had not changed. She tried the overhead lights and could not get them to work. So she was entirely dependent on the flashlight. Since she'd made the journey before, she was able to find her way to the wine cellar. There she stood for a moment, perplexed.

Why had she come down to this isolated place where she had first seen the ghost? Because of what Inspector Halliday had said. She had a genuine desire to find the secret passage. If it joined with the one leading to Lady Madeline Smith's house, a great deal might be explained. Nocturnal visitors might well have made use of the passage.

The shadows pressed in on her ominously, and she recalled the unpleasant experience with the bat when she'd been down there with Edward. And this made her consider further. Bats usually came from the outside. They would not originate in cellars. So there must be a lost passage!

She moved beyond the wine cellar to an area where the walls seemed merely rough-hewn rock. The sound of running water seemed louder. She followed the sound.

And suddenly she found herself staring at a narrow passage in the rocky wall, not much more than a slit about a foot thick and perhaps six feet high. Could this be the passage?

She flashed the beam of the flashlight on it and saw that the rock had great thickness. Then she moved toward it sideways and tried to edge her body through the dark slit. She was surprised that she could go through it sideways with ease. It was apparently wider than she'd judged.

After a moment she emerged in a tunnel with a higher roof and jagged walls. She felt her heart pounding as she advanced in this unknown dark place, and kept the beam of the flashlight ahead to find the way. As she allowed its light to flow over the walls, it suddenly fixed on something that froze her where she stood. Edward's face gazing at her from the wall of the tunnel, and his name in large letters underneath!

Chapter Ten

Vanessa screamed, and her scream echoed mockingly through the tunnel's deep recesses. The flashlight dropped from her hand, and its lamp broke on the floor by her feet. With a sob she bent to retrieve it—too late. Now she straightened up and stared into the ghostly blackness. She had seen Edward's face as if it were molded in stone. Had it been an apparition, or were her nerves playing tricks on her again?

She stood there trembling, not knowing what to do. She was by no means sure that she could find her way back in the darkness. She was lost down here in this maze of passages. She might die down here in this secret place without anyone knowing it.

If she went on, she had no idea where the tunnel might lead. Hopefully to Lady Madeline Smith's house, but there was no being sure of this. If she tried to find her way back, she might take a wrong turning or even be caught in that narrow slit of a passage. Without the flashlight, she was in a truly desperate plight.

To top that, there was the knowledge that somewhere there in the distance she had seen that ghostly face! The face of her dead husband! What did it mean? Low sobs came from between her chattering teeth, and she stood there wavering between one frightening choice and another.

At last she decided to retrace her steps, and she turned and began moving along slowly in the pitch blackness. The darkness was itself like a wall, and she made her penetration of it with hesitancy.

Then she halted at the sight of what seemed a tiny ray of bright light. This was followed by a weird cry that reverberated in the tunnel. Her terror increased, and she remained frozen there as the glow increased, and she tried to guess what it was. It slowly came closer to her.

Then she heard more clearly, "Anyone there?"

"Here!" she cried. "I'm here!"

"Coming!" the voice echoed hollowly.

Now she saw the bright beam of a flashlight like the one she had broken coming toward her, and a moment later she was able to make out the figure of the bald manservant, Norris.

"Norris!" she exclaimed in relief.

The bald man joined her and in his polite manner said, "I very nearly didn't find you!"

"How did you know I was here?" she asked.

"I happened to be at the end of the hallway when you went down the cellar stairs," Norris said. "When you didn't return, I began to worry. I decided to arm myself with a flashlight and follow you."

"I'm so glad you did!"

"But I very nearly missed you," he said. "I happened to be by that slit in the wall when I heard your scream from the tunnel on the other side."

"I screamed because I saw something that frightened me," she said.

"Not surprising, in this place, your ladyship," Norris

said, becoming more formal as he regained his poise.

"I wanted to find the secret passage."

"And you have," Norris informed her. "Though I must say, your ladyship, I can't see what benefit you will get from it."

"My husband told me about it, but he didn't know where it was."

Norris nodded. "Mr. Edward's mother did not wish him to know as a lad. She was afraid he might get in trouble down here. Nor was Mr. Leonard told of its location, though the judge and his wife know about it."

"The entrance to it is very deceptive. It seems smaller than it is."

"An optical illusion, your ladyship."

Fear crossed her lovely face as she remembered what had made her scream. "I had a bad fright," she told the servant. "I saw what seemed a ghost."

"Indeed, your ladyship?" Norris lost none of his calm in spite of her obvious terror.

She turned and pointed. "It was down there. I saw a face. My husband's face! He seemed to be staring at me from the wall, and his name was etched out on the wall under his face."

Norris gave her an odd look. "I think I may be able to offer an explanation," he said.

"I don't see how."

"Come with me," he said. And he began walking toward the spot where she had seen the ghostly face.

She followed him, still in a shattered state. "On the left," she said.

"Yes, I think so," Norris said absently, and he ran the beam of his flashlight over the wall until he came upon the face.

189

"That's it!" she exclaimed.

"I thought so!"

"What does it mean?"

"If you will look closely, Lady Norville, you will see that the face is part of a tomb. It is a likeness of an Edward Norville who lived years ago and whom our Sir Edward resembled. The tomb was installed here years ago when the Norvilles of that time decided to use the tunnel as a sort of catacomb for family burials."

"But they did not continue with it?"

"No. The idea was repugnant to the next Lord Norville, so this lone tomb with the bodies of that long-ago Edward Norville and his wife remains deep below ground here."

The disclosure fascinated Vanessa at the same time that it sent a cold shiver down her spine. She peered at the mold-covered face and commented, "The face must have been sculptured by someone of great talent."

"I agree," Norris said respectfully as he continued to shine the flashlight's beam on the sculpture that had given her such a start. "There is no record of who completed it, and now the edges of the tomb have been covered with mold and decay so that they merge with the tunnel wall itself."

She glanced at the bald man. "Let me ask one more question."

"By all means."

"How did they get the bodies down here? Not through that small passage by which we came, surely?"

"No, your ladyship," Norris said. "They came from the other end of the tunnel."

"The other end?"

"It leads from the Smith house, next door," the man-servant explained. "In those days, both houses were owned by the Norville family. So there was no problem bringing the bodies and caskets down that way.''

Vanessa recalled what the inspector had said to her about the tunnels being used as an escape route by the murderer of her husband. And it seemed to her they might also prove convenient for anyone wanting access to the old mansion.

She asked, "Does the passage to Lady Madeline Smith's house still exist?"

"Yes," Norris said. "Though, to the best of my knowledge, it is never used."

"I understand," she said quietly, and glancing down the tunnel in the direction of the passage to the Smith house, she gave a tiny involuntary shudder.

Norris at once said, "You will get a chill down here, your ladyship. You shouldn't linger here."

"You're probably right, Norris, I was foolish to come down here alone in the first place. Thank you for coming for me."

"Not at all," the bald man said as he began escorting her back.

"At least my foolish curiosity has been satisfied," she tolb him as they walked along the tunnel in the darkness.

When they reached the passage giving access to the Norville House cellar, she again slid her body through it sideways. And she realized that Norris was right, the passage was deceiving. It was a good deal wider than she had first guessed.

Norris saw her safely to the ground floor of the main house and then discreetly excused himself. She was still a trifle shocked from her eerie experience in the dark depths under the old mansion, and she resolved never to go there alone again.

When she went downstairs for dinner that evening, Judge James Norville was waiting to talk with her. Over the usual before-dinner drink he took her aside.

"Edward's lawyers were in touch with me today," he informed her.

"Oh?"

The stout man nodded solemnly. "There are many matters to be dealt with regarding the estate. Perhaps number one on the list is the stables."

"They want to know what to do with them?" she asked.

"Yes," Judge Norville said. "Neither Leonard nor I am interested in taking over their supervision. Unless you want to become active in the racing world, the best solution would be to sell the horses."

Sadness swept through her, and a slight frown showed on her lovely face. "Edward gave so much of himself to the stables. I hate to dispose of them, and yet I have no desire to operate them."

"Exactly," Sir James said. "Your pregnancy will in time cut down on your activity. I think it would be most unsuitable for you to try to keep the horses."

"What did the lawyers suggest?"

"They want you to decide," the judge said. "I imagine one solution would be to publicly auction off the stables."

"If we could only sell them to a friend of Edward's," she said. "Perhaps that would be best."

"Any ideas of who might be interested?" the old man asked.

Her face suddenly brightened. "Augustus Gordon!" she exclaimed.

The round, crimson face of the judge showed mild surprise. "The actor?"

"Yes. He has often told me he'd like to live the sort of life Edward lived. And he shared Edward's interest in racing, though I don't think he has any horses of his own."

Would he have sufficient money?"

"I hadn't thought about that."

"You'd better," the judge advised. "It takes a great deal of money to own and operate a stable."

Vanessa considered. "I'm sure that is true. But Augustus Gordon is one of the big names in stage and films. I'd expect he has enough money."

"Perhaps," the old man conceded.

"Let me discuss it with him before we do anything," she suggested.

"By all means," the judge said. "You can let me know."

When they finished their discussion, they joined the others. Vanessa was slightly uneasy to see that Lady Madeline Smith was a dinner guest once again. The tall, beautiful girl with the glacial manner was seated in conversation with the equally cold Lady Norville. The sometime invalid had appeared in honor of this guest of whom she so obviously approved. Leonard hovered in the background with his mother. When he saw his father and Vanessa coming back into the living room, he came up to meet them.

He smiled for Vanessa's benefit. "You look lovely tonight in that gray dress. I'm glad to see you finally discarding black."

"Thank you," she said. "I see you have a guest."

"Madeline," he said lightly. "Yes. I'm taking her to a party some of my BBC friends are giving tonight. I'd like to have you come one night. They are mostly people with a theater background. You'd like them.''

"That would be nice, sometime," she said, emphasizing the "sometime." She could not help but think of the change in him since their first meeting. This sleek, rather good-looking young man in his velvet dinner jacket and black tie was a far cry from the shaggy creature who had lived in Soho.

"I'd have asked you tonight, but I was afraid you would think it too soon after all that has happened," the young man said awkwardly.

She gave him a wan smile. "You were right. And please go back to Madeline and don't pay any more attention to me. I can see her and Lady Norville watching us now with critical eyes."

"I don't care!" Leonard said.

"I do!" Vanessa insisted. "Go pay attention to your date while I speak with your mother."

"You're a strange one!" Leonard said with a wry smile. But he did obey her and wander over to Madeline and Lady Norville, both of whom at once relaxed. Vanessa went to the other side of the fireplace, where Edith Norville and her husband, the judge, were standing.

Edith Norville gave her a pleasant nod. "I see my son has deserted you for Madeline."

In a low voice Vanessa said, "Lady Norville approves of Lady Madeline as she does no one else. I think she is playing matchmaker again."

"That is too bad," Edith Norville said, "since I'm almost certain Leonard will disappoint her. He is one to make his own decisions."

"All too true," the judge agreed.

"I hope that he does," Vanessa said, her cheeks warming. She had not wanted to make it seem that she was interested in Leonard, though she feared they might have taken it that way. She only worried that the cold Lady Madeline would hardly make him a suitable wife.

Dinner was something of an ordeal. Fortunately Leonard and Lady Madeline left soon afterward for the party. And Lady Norville took this as her cue to wish everyone good night and vanish. She had become something of a recluse since Edward's murder. Vanessa had barely spoken to her all evening, and not once did the older woman make any reference to the grandchild whom Vanessa would give birth to in a few months. Her hatred of Vanessa seemed to have already extended to the unborn child.

Vanessa remained with Edith and Judge Norville for about a half-hour longer and then went up to her apartment. It troubled her that she could no longer feel safe in it. She knew that Augustus Gordon's advice had been sensible. She should leave the old mansion. In an apartment of her own she would feel much more secure. Perhaps when her father returned from America he could find a house in Stratford where she might live until she had the baby. The prospect of having her father for company was a cheering one. But opposed to it was her worry that Edward would wish her to remain at Norville Hall.

She stood by the window staring out at Blake Square where Edward had been murdered. Who had wielded the knife that had struck him down? What had happened to it? Her eyes wandered to the mansion owned by the parents of Lady Madeline Smith. And once again a monstrous thought went through her mind. Could Madeline have been the killer? Was that how such an easy escape had been made by the culprit? Inspector Halliday had made some discreet comments about the passage at the Smith mansion joining with the other tunnels. An ideal escape route.

Now Madeline was suddenly so friendly with Leonard. Could the two have been in it together? Were they still plotting and waiting for the moment to be rid of her and the child still unborn? Yet Leonard had come to her aid the night of her fall. But he had protested against the possibility of her having seen a ghost, and he had counseled her to say nothing about it to anyone. Could it be because he was mixed up in a plot against her?

Was she alone in this grim old mansion in her stand against all of them? Were they determined to rid the house of Norville of the latest in the tragic line of Capricorn brides? Was this their way of combating the ancient curse? Debating the possibility left her mind in a troubled chaos.

She let the drape fall across the window again as she turned from her study of the dark night. As she moved across the room to her dresser, the phone suddenly began to ring. The sound of it made her start. And she wondered why she should be fearful of such a common sound as the ringing of the phone. Yet she was.

The phone was on a small desk in the bedroom near the door leading to the living room. She went and picked it up, to hear the familiar voice of Augustus Gordon. The star said, "Is that you, Vanessa?"

"Yes."

"You were a long time answering."

"I wasn't near the phone."

"You weren't asleep?"

"No."

He seemed worried. "You don't sound yourself. Is there anything wrong?"

"No," she said. "I was thinking. My mind was miles away."

"You're sure you're all right?"

"I'm sure!"

"I hope so," he said dubiously. "I phoned because I felt our luncheon didn't go all that well. That maybe I bullied you too much, trying to get you to leave that place. Which I still think you should do."

"I enjoyed seeing you," she said.

"I want it to be always that way," Gus assured her. "I want us always to be the best of friends."

"We shall be."

"Forgive me for calling so late," the star said. "But it was on my mind."

"I'm glad you called," she said. "I want to see you. I have something to discuss with you. A business matter."

The voice at the other end of the line warmed. "Sounds intriguing."

"When and where shall we meet?" she asked. "I want to take *you* to lunch this time."

The star laughed. "Whatever you say! I don't mind being a kept man. I have to visit the wig shop tomorrow morning. Why don't we meet at John Fitzgibbon's just before noon, and then move on from there."

"I'd like that," she said. "I enjoy the atmosphere of the old shop. It makes me think of theater."

"It is completely theater," Gus told her. "For a one-man establishment, he does a huge wig-and-costume business."

"I'll be there just before twelve," she promised. They said their good nights, and she hung up. The prospect of meeting the star again and discussing the sale of the stables with him gave her something to look forward to. And so she prepared for bed in a better frame of mind.

Perhaps because of this, she went to sleep almost at once and slept soundly all night. She awoke in the morning without any nightmares to haunt her and feeling much more like her old self. As usual, she had a slight bit of morning sickness, but the doctor had assured her this would vanish after another month or so.

As a surprise for Gus she phoned the Dorchester on her own and had a table reserved for them. She wore her smartest new suit of dark navy, and her gray fur coat and matching beret. Edith saw her on the way out and made some admiring comments about her appearance. Vanessa thus left the house in a good mood.

The narrow side street in which the wigmaker's shop was located was heavy with traffic on this fine morning in early spring. The taxi driver had to let her out a few doors from the entrance to the shop. She paid him and hurried onto the sidewalk.

Gus Gordon was already there, talking with the jovial John Fitzgibbon. They both greeted her warmly, and she moved about the dark old shop with its balcony in the rear, studying the various costumes and wigs on display. Then she paused before a bulletin board. There was one notice on the board that caught her attention more than the others.

She turned to Gus and called the well-dressed actor over. "Come here and see this!"

Good-naturedly he joined her and asked, "What?"

"This notice. There's a small studio theater for hire on the top floor of a building in the theater district. Just the place for a theater club. It even has a bar."

"So?" the star said.

She turned to him with excited eyes. "This is some-

198

thing I could do! I have the money now. I could hire that studio, get together a half-dozen actors, and do some suitable play. I could be director and run the club. There are dozens of them all over London, and many of them are doing well."

Augustus Gordon protested. "You don't belong in some attic theater club. You should be on the West End stage. And you can be, whenever you want."

"I can't be until after the baby!" she reminded him. "In the meantime, I could work on this project, and it would be good for me. I'd be giving actors work. We might do enough business between club memberships and selling drinks to pay our way. I wouldn't mind, in any case. I'd be in the theater again!"

The star shrugged. "You can't count on making money, or even breaking even. But I forget you're a wealthy woman now."

"I will be when the estate is fully settled," she said. "In the meantime, I'm sure I could get my lawyers to give me enough capital for this venture."

The wigmaker had overheard her, and he rubbed his hands gleefully. "And John Fitzgibbon will supply the costumes!"

"Why not?" She laughed. "And what would you suggest to start the venture?"

The wigmaker considered this as he scratched his chin. Then he seemed to have a sudden inspiration. "I know the very thing," he exclaimed. "A musical version of *Tom Jones*. I have the whole production—costumes, scenic drapes, and wigs. I put the package together for a company in Bristol that never did get started. Everything's together and ready!"

"Tom Jones!" Vanessa said. "I saw the film, and I

think a musical version would be grand! Is it a large-cast version?"

"No," the wigmaker said. "Only eight principals and a few extras. And I know the studio that is available for rent. I'm sure you'd like it. It is clean, and a good size. Fine little stage."

Augustus Gordon said, "But it is in the attic. How many steps up to it?"

The old wigmaker looked a trifle uneasy. "It is a long way up. But the fire authorities have licensed it, so it's safe."

"But not good for the elderly or heart patients, I'd say," was the star's comment.

Vanessa picked up the conversation again with Capricorn zeal. She said, "The small club theaters appeal to young people who can afford their prices better than the West End. So I don't think the stairs would matter."

Augustus Gordon stared at her in surprise. "You are really serious about this?"

"I am," she said. "I'm going to write down the phone number and address. I'll speak to my lawyers about it."

Old John Fitzgibbon said, "And I have a copy of the play and music. I'll get it so you can study it at your ease." And he waddled off to find it.

The star warned her, "I think old John is encouraging us just to get some costumes rented."

She smiled. "I don't care. It does interest me. And I do need something."

"I thought I was the one you wanted to discuss business with," Augustus Gordon said.

"You are, and I have our table reserved for lunch," she said. "If I decide to go ahead with the theater club, you can help me with it as well."

The star raised a protesting hand. "Not a chance! I'm preparing a production for the West End. That is going to take all my time. Now, where are we going for luncheon?"

"The Dorchester," she said proudly. "You aren't the only one to book a table there."

As soon as old John Fitzgibbon returned with a copy of the book and music for her, they left. The old man informed her that the building with the attic theater was no more than a block from his shop. If she hadn't had the luncheon table reserved, she would have taken time to go and look at the studio right away. But they were already a few minutes late for their reservation.

At the Dorchester she told Augustus Gordon of her problem. "We have to sell the horses," she said. "And I thought of you."

"Me?" he asked in astonishment.

"You always said you'd like to own your own racing stable, like Edward. Here is your chance."

The actor smiled at her across the table. "You're very ambitious for me!"

"I know Edward would like you to have the horses."

"Why can't you keep them? You say money is no object with you in starting a theater club."

"That's different," she said. "I can do the theater-club thing myself and enjoy it. I don't know anything about racing."

"You can hire a manager."

"I don't want to," she said. And then a shadow crossed her lovely face. "I'll be honest. I think something came out of racing to cause Edward's murder. Perhaps it was that Hawkins? Who knows?"

The star said, "I have been told the police think Hawkins left the country right after the murder. So you could be right.''

"I think I am.''

Augustus Gordon gave her a knowing glance. "Yet, by your account, Lady Norville and the family blame it on the curse of the Brides of Saturn! Blame him for taking on a Capricorn wife."

"That's something I don't want to discuss," she said. "What about the horses? Will you take over the stable?"

Augustus Gordon sat back in his chair and stared at her across the white-clothed table with a rueful expression on his longish handsome face. "Have you any idea how wealthy I am?"

"No."

"Well, I'm not nearly so wealthy as you might like to think."

"You have earned big money as a star."

"And I've spent nearly all of it," the famous actor said with a shrug. "In fact, I need to work right away or I'll be going into debt."

Vanessa said, "I had no idea. I'm sorry."

"You should have known. Your father is an actor."

"But never a famous one! Your name is so well-known!"

The star smiled ruefully. "I have fame, but alas, no fortune. I can't buy the stable. But I tell you what. I would like to own a part of it. I think I can scrape enough money together to buy Flying Anne and race her, if you'll let me buy just one horse."

"Of course!" she said. "Edward would want you to have her."

"Don't agree too readily," the actor warned her. "Your lawyers may not approve. They will want to auction the stables to the highest bidder, and the highest bidder may insist on getting Flying Anne in the transaction.''

''No,'' she said. ''I will stipulate she is to be sold to you. I can arrange it.''

''Wonderful!'' Augustus Gordon said. ''Let me know the price, and I'll arrange for the purchase.''

Her green, almond-shaped eyes were bright. ''The price will be one hundred pounds.''

''One hundred pounds!'' The star gasped. ''Flying Anne is worth thousands!''

''But I name the price, and it will be one hundred pounds,'' she told him.

Augustus Gordon reached across the table to take her hand in his, and in a voice filled with emotion he said, ''It is fitting that I receive a thoroughbred through the kindness of a thoroughbred! Thank you, darling!''

The luncheon was a huge success. When it was over, Augustus Gordon had to rush off to a rehearsal of his new show. He left her in the lobby of the Dorchester to have the doorman find her a cab. It was then she had an impulse to call Leonard at the BBC and speak to him about her theater-club idea. She was still full of it.

She reached him on the pay phone after an expected amount of delay. Leonard was both surprised to hear from her and interested in her suggested project.

He said, ''I think you should look into it. You need something like this!''

''Perhaps you might give me some help,'' she ventured.

''Anything I can do,'' the young man said.

''Could you get away for a little this afternoon and look at the place with me?''

"Yes," he said. "I can meet you in an hour. Where?"

"Let's meet at Fitzgibbon's, the wigmaker. He is the one who had the sign about it on his bulletin board. And the studio is in a building not far from his place."

"I know Fitzgibbon's," Leonard said. "I'll meet you there at four."

And so it all began. She and Leonard climbed the many stairs to the attic theater, but when they reached it, they felt repaid for their efforts. It was brightly painted, with an auditorium that would hold eighty, and a fair-sized stage, well-equipped. In an adjoining room there was a bar, and chairs for use for cards or other games. Dart boards were on the walls in the publike atmosphere of the place.

The little man in the bowler hat who gave them a tour of the place finally said, "Well, you've seen it all. What do you think?"

Vanessa said, "Why did the previous club give it up?"

"Fellow who was the main one in the group found a job in Italy in films. There was no one else with the money or energy to make a go of it after he left," the little man said.

Vanessa glanced at Leonard. "What do you think?"

"It's a dream of a little theater for those who can survive the stairs," he said.

"I agree," Vanessa said, feeling happier than she had in months, the glow of her theater days returning to help fill the void she'd known in her loss of Edward. She told the little man in the bowler hat, "I'll have my lawyers phone you. I'm almost sure I'll be taking it over."

"You'll never regret it, Lady Norville," the little man assured her. "Only needs someone with get-up and go to make it a gold mine!"

Leonard chuckled. "A gold mine in the sky! That's what we are all looking for."

When they left the building, Leonard found a cab. They were both excited, and discussed the project as the cab headed for Blake Square.

Leonard suddenly changed his tone and said, "There's just one thing."

"What?"

The young scenic artist said, "Don't mention this to Lady Norville."

"Oh? You think she would try to stop me?"

"I know she would," he warned. "She hates everything to do with the theater. She'd object strongly to this. If you keep it quiet, and the lawyers approve, you'll be on solid ground. But don't let her guess anything about it until you have it all arranged."

"Thanks, Leonard," she said, gazing at him fondly in the simidarkness of the cab's rear seat.

"I know you're excited about this, but you'll have to hide your feelings at Norville House tonight and until you have everything settled."

"I'll be discreet," she promised.

And she was. Though she was fairly bubbling with happiness, she forced herself to be outwardly reserved. Every now and then Leonard would catch her eye at the table, and she feared she might give her secret away. But she managed to preserve a calm front.

She went up to her apartment early and went to bed to read the book of *Tom Jones* and study the music. She intended to see her lawyers the next day and discuss the sale of the stables and her taking over the theater. So she immersed herself in the script, and before she knew it, the hours had scurried by and it was past midnight.

With a satisfied sigh she put the script aside and turned out the lights. Again she fell asleep quickly. But on this night her sleep was to be broken. It seemed to her she had barely closed her eyes when she heard a voice calling her name in a ghostly fashion.

Chapter Eleven

The voice was flat and sexless, and it seemed to be coming from the living room. Vanessa sat up in bed and came more fully awake. She groped for the bedside lamp and turned it on.

"Vanessa!" the voice intoned again.

Fear was already rising in her as she ventured to call in return, "Who is it?"

"Vanessa!" It came again with a ghostly sameness.

Frightened to remain in bed, and terrified of what the weird voice calling her name might signify, she debated what to do. Her decision was to go and investigate the voice. It occurred to her it might be Edith Norville with some sort of problem. Perhaps Lady Norville was ill, or the judge. This possibility eased some of her fright, and she went across to the living-room door and opened it.

"Vanessa!" Now the phantom voice was coming from the small kitchen on the other side of the living room.

She ventured a step into the living room and turned on one of the table lamps. Standing there in a tense state, she called out, "I'm here in the living room. What do you want?"

There was only silence. This made her more nervous. Cautiously she made her way to the swinging door leading from the dining room to the kitchen. She pushed open the door, and then in the light from the living room she saw the ghost!

It was the same bent figure in brown with the shawl covering a good part of the creature's wizened, ugly face! The phantom snarled at her and raised a bony hand with something in it. Vanessa cried out and tried to step back, but didn't manage it in time. She saw the hand come down, and felt something hit her head hard. She moaned and slumped down onto the floor unconscious.

She reached out with her hand to grasp something, but there was nothing she could hold onto. She was drowning in some strange place, unable to breathe, her lungs gradually filling with water! She now struggled to find something by which she could drag herself out of the water, save herself from drowning, and she grasped only air!

Moaning a little, Vanessa turned over on her side. And she realized she was on the hardwood floor, not in some river or lake. She was on the floor, and she could not breathe! Weakly she raised herself just a little and then fell back. She had a dreadful pain in her head, and she was so weak. So terribly weak!

Now she raised herself a little again and began slowly to drag herself across the floog to the swinging door. When she reached it, she lowered her head again and sobbed. But after a brief pause she summoned the strength and reason to push back the door and make her way into the living room. The swinging door closed behind her, and she lay on the living-room rug gasping.

It took a little while. She didn't know how long. But at last she got to her knees, then stood up and staggered across the room to the phone. She knew Leonard's number, and with shaking fingers she dialed it. Then she waited as it rang many times.

He finally answered sleepily, "Yes?"

"Leonard! I'm in trouble!" she gasped.

"Vanessa! What is it?" he said, coming awake at once.

"Please come! I'll open the door," she managed.

"I'll be there in a moment," he promised.

Wearily she returned the phone to its cradle and then staggered across the room and unlocked the door to the hallway. This major accomplishment managed in her frail state, she slumped down into the nearest easy chair and held her head in her hands.hThe room was swimming around her, and she could not seem to get her thoughts straightened out.

Footsteps in the corridor, and the door burst open. An upset Leonard came rushing to her side. "Vanessa? What the devil?" He asked this question almost to himself, and turned and stared in the direction of the kitchen. Then he raced out there.

She raised her eyes, to see him vanish through the swinging door. Next she heard the sound of windows being opened, and after a moment he came back in the room gasping.

He stared at her from the middle of the room. "Did you do that?"

"What?"

"Turn the gas on! The range was wide open, and the room full of the stuff! I've turned it off and opened all the windows out there." He came striding toward her. "What made you do this . . . try to kill yourself?"

She pressed her hands to her temples and groaned. "I didn't!" she moaned. "I didn't do it!"

"You didn't do it?" He sounded dubious.

"No," she managed weakly. "Someone called me out

there. I saw the ghost! The witch! She struck me with something, and when I came to, I thought I was drowning. I was on the floor.''

"Vanessa!" the young man reproved her. "You don't have to lie to me. We're good friends. I'll understand if you tell me a despondent mood came over you and you tried to kill yourself.''

"But I didn't!" she protested unhappily.

Leonard was standing above her. "You're telling me that some sort of phantom came in here and lured you to the kitchen, knocked you out, and then turned on the gas so you'd die there?''

"Yes!" She touched the bump on her head. "Feel the bump! It's real enough.''

He came close and gingerly ran his fingers over the part of her skull that she'd indicated. His fingers found the bump and touched it lightly.

"You do have a bump," he reluctantly admitted.

"I told you!"

He eyed her suspiciously. "I don't know, Vanessa. You could have gotten that in your fall.''

"How can I prove to you the witch was there? It's the curse of the Brides of Saturn working again!''

He waved a hand in a tired attempt to dismiss this. With a sigh he told her, "No matter how it happened, you've come through it. And in a little while the kitchen will have been aired out enough.''

She looked at him in despair. "You think I'm suffering from another nightmare! Or that I tried to commit suicide!''

"I honestly don't know what to think," he admitted. "I'm only grateful that you called me and that you're safe.''

Her eyes met his. "Either the phantom or someone in this house is trying to kill me! Kill me and my baby!"

He stared at her worriedly. "I'll see how things are in the kitchen," he said. And he hurried off through the swinging doors again.

She sat there in the chair, hardly able to believe what was going on. Certainly Leonard didn't believe her story. He was suspicious of a suicide attempt on her part. And she knew the evidence suggested that. How could she expect him to accept her ridiculous story? How could she expect anyone to accept it?

Leonard came back and said, "Everything is fine out there now. In the future, be careful about turning on that range and not lighting the burners. The whole house could have been blown up."

"I felt so ill when I came to."

"Not much wonder," the young man said grimly. "I don't know why you're not dead. Do you have any sleeping tablets on hand?"

"Yes."

"I want you to take a couple while I'm here. Then I'll wait in one of the living-room chairs until I'm sure you're asleep. In the morning you'd better have Dr. Mosher see you."

"No!"

"We'll argue about that later," he said with a sigh. "Right now I want you to get the sleeping tablets and let me see you take them."

She rose shakily. "There's no need. I'll be all right."

He took her by the arm. "No. I want to see you safely in bed and asleep."

So she did what he asked, without any more argument. He stood beside her bed and tucked her in. Then he bent and kissed her on the forehead. He said, "I'll be resting in a chair in the living room. If you want me, call out."

She looked up at him gratefully, her eyes dulled by weariness. "You are good to me, Leonard," she said with a sigh. Then she closed her eyes.

When she opened them again, it was another day. The crisis was over. The maid came with her breakfast and prepared tea in the kitchen. It was as if nothing had ever happened. She had only the bump on her head and a feeling of weariness to remind her of those terrifying moments in the kitchen.

By the time she went downstairs, Leonard had gone. There was no one else she dared to discuss the incident with. So she tried to put it out of her mind, and began the day's schedule. A phone call to the lawyers' offices resulted in an early-afternoon appointment. This would be the high spot of her day. She carefully placed the play manuscript and music in an envelope to take with her.

A letter arrived by airmail from New York. It was from her father, and he wrote her that he would be arriving in England a few days after she received the letter. This was good news, as she had not been sure when to expect him. At least now she had a rough idea of his time of arrival. She had so much to tell him, she could hardly wait to see him.

She reached the lawyers' offices a few minutes ahead of her appointment. But Mr. Snodgrass, the senior partner, graciously let her into his private office a little early. He was a tall, rugged man in his sixties, with bushy white hair and a stern face dominated by a high forehead.

He patiently listened to her several requests regarding the estate. When she had finished, he cleared his throat and said, "Well, you haven't asked for the impossible.

212

And I think you are wise to sell the stables.''

"I feel it best," she said.

"So do I," Mr. Snodgrass agreed. He frowned slightly as he continued, "Your offering Flying Anne to Mr. Gordon for the ridiculous sum of one hundred pounds is very generous. But do you feel it wise?"

"I don't care," she said. "Edward and Augustus Gordon were close friends. They often went to the racetrack together."

"I realize that," the old lawyer said. "Have it as you wish. I'll prepare the papers of sale for Mr. Gordon. I suggest we put the rest of the stable up for auction. It will take a month or more to get ready for the sale."

"Do as you think best," she said. "I'd like to get busy with the theater-club venture."

The eyes under the bushy white brows were anxious. "You are sure the project won't tax you too much?"

"No," she said. "Leonard Norville has agreed to help me."

"I see," the old lawyer said. "So you wish us to contact the owners of the studio and rent it?"

"Yes."

"For how long?"

She had it all thought out. "Rent it for a year, with a yearly option to renew. And stipulate there be no rent raise in the renewals for at least three years."

Mr. Snodgrass eyed her with approval. "You have a good head for business, young woman."

"Thank you," she said. "I hope to be able to prove that to you. I'm sure I can operate the theater club and show a profit."

"I hope so," the lawyer said dryly. "We might be criticized as executors of the estate if you fail."

"I'll not fail," she promised. "Just see that I have a sufficient amount in my account to work with, and have the rental agreements signed as I suggested."

The lawyer showed interest. "You have had training and experience in the theater, Lady Norville?"

"Yes."

"It should be a fine project for you."

"I think it will be a great help to me. I have been terribly nervous since my husband's murder.

The stern face showed sympathy. "Not much wonder. A dreadful thing!"

"It was," she said quietly. "And I fear they will never find the killer or killers."

"At least he left you to carry on," the lawyer said. "And you are to have a child. An heir to the title."

She gave the old lawyer a questioning look. "If anything happened to me, and the child was not born, who would get the title?"

Mr. Snodgrass showed embarrassment. "Nothing is going to happen to you, of course."

"But suppose it should," she persisted. "Who gets the title then?"

"I honestly don't know."

"You don't know?" she echoed in surprise.

"No. The late Lord Norville, your husband's father, was a complex man. One given to secrets. He enjoyed keeping things to himself. Before he died, he gave my uncle, then the head of the firm, a sealed envelope. His instructions were that it was to be opened only in the event his son died without a wife or an heir."

"That is very strange."

214

"I agree. It amounts to a secret will. But it is quite within the law."

"And you still have the envelope?"

"Yes. It is not to be destroyed until the succession through your late husband is assured."

"We will not have to wait many months for that," was her reply.

"I hope you have a son," the lawyer said.

"So do I," she agreed. "But I wouldn't reject a girl who was Edward's daughter."

"Certainly not," the lawyer agreed. "Is there anything else I can do for you, Lady Norville?"

"I think not," she said, rising. "You have been most kind."

"It is what we are paid for, my lady," the senior partner of the law firm said. And he rose to see her on her way.

For several days and nights everything went so well for her that she began to believe the attack on her in the kitchen had been a bad dream and nothing more.

She began work at the attic theater. A call to British Equity lined up a number of young theater people as prospects for her production of *Tom Jones*. Leonard entered into the effort with great enthusiasm. And old John Fitzgibbon thought himself the father of the project.

"Never would have come about but for the sign on my bulletin board," he repeated gleefully to anyone who would listen. And he insisted on giving both Vanessa and Leonard keys to the wig shop. "I often give them out to people I trust," he told them. "There are times when I'm away from the shop, and I would not want either of you to be locked out."

Because they often met at the ancient wig shop before moving on to the attic theater club, they accepted the keys and occasionally used them. Vanessa was alone at the club one morning going over accounts and waiting for the man who was to be club steward to appear. She was going over the cost of the bar stock when she heard someone knock at the door.

She went over and opened it, to see her father standing there with a smile on his face. "John Fitzgibbon told me I'd find you here. I had called Norville House, and they said you were out and to try the wig shop."

Vanessa kissed and hugged her father enthusiastically and then led him in to inspect the club. She said, "It is a ruse I'm using for a while. I don't want Lady Norville to find out I'm going to operate this place until we open."

"Why not?" her handsome father asked.

She shrugged. "Lady Norville doesn't approve of the theater."

Her father looked surprised. "Then how did she ever come to accept you as her daughter-in-law?"

"I'm not sure that she has," was Vanessa's wry reply.

"You worry me," James Masters said. "Maybe you should have considered before starting this place."

She was holding one of his hands in hers as she led him about the place. "If I had, I never would have had it. I now have full backing of the estate lawyers, and Edward's cousin, Leonard, is giving all his spare time to getting the club started. Rehearsals begin in a few days. Meanwhile, I'm supposed to be working part-time for Mr. Fitzgibbon."

Her father shook his head. "I must say, it is all very confusing to me."

"There are other things to confuse you," she promised him. "But let me show you the small auditorium and the

216

stage before we do any more talking. I want to see if you like them.''

James Masters let her show him every corner of the attic theater. He then expressed his approval of it, and they sat down for a more serious conversation.

They sat in the small room she had fixed up as her office. It contained only a desk, a filing cabinet, and the two chairs in which they were seated. She was glad that their meeting had come at the theater club rather than in Norville House. Here they had complete privacy.

She told her father solemnly, ''I worry that they have not found Edward's killer.''

''I'm sure you do,'' he agreed. ''A nasty business. Poor Edward!''

''There is more than that,'' she went on. ''I think whoever murdered Edward is trying to kill me.''

''Vanessa!'' Her father looked shocked.

''It's true,'' she said. ''I've told you about the legendary family curse, the curse of the Brides of Saturn. Because of a superstitious belief in this, Lady Norville and some others in the family think I'm to blame for what happened. Tragedy always is supposed to follow when an heir to the Norville title marries a girl born under the sign of Capricorn.''

''Ridiculous nonsense!'' her father scoffed.

''Not to them, I'm afraid.'' She sighed. ''And that has helped confuse the matter.''

''Go on.''

''It's a long story,'' she warned him.

''I want to hear all of it,'' he insisted.

So she told him, beginning with her first sighting the ghost in the cellar of Norville House and ending with the latest attack on her in the kitchen of her apartment.

James Masters stood up and began pacing in the small office. He glanced at her worriedly and said, "Unless you are suffering from some sort of mental breakdown, you are being pursued by a killer."

"Or the phantom?"

"Let us forget all about that silly curse," her father said. "It seems to me that you may be dealing with one of the family. Or maybe this Lady Madeline Smith whom you suspect had a serious quarrel with Edward."

"I'm almost certain they had a bad quarrel," she agreed.

"You heard the voice of your attacker the night you were left in the kitchen to die."

"Yes."

Her father paused and stared at her. "You have had theater training. You've been taught to mimic and identify voices. Can't you offer some hint as to who it was you heard?"

"I've tried to place the voice," she said. "It was cleverly done. Almost impossible to say who it was."

"I'm surprised. Voices are hard to disguise. And we assume whoever our culprit is, he has not had your training."

"I know," she said. "I'm almost sure whoever it is will try to kill me at some future time. But I have no idea when or how. It's terrifying."

Her father stood scowling at her. "Then why in heaven's name don't you get out of Norville House? Away from London. Come to Stratford with me until the child is born."

She nodded. "I'd thought of that. But I've decided against it."

"Why?"

"I think Edward would want me to remain at Norville House. And I believe it is the only way I can trap the killer into coming out into the open to be identified."

"Much good it will do you to identify him and be killed for your efforts," James Masters sputtered. "I don't see how, as your only living parent, I can desert you in a situation like this. I think you should come with me and let me protect you."

"I have Leonard," she said.

Her father groaned. "Has it ever struck you that this Leonard could himself be the killer? That he is likely the next in line to the title if you and the baby are eliminated?"

"Yes. I've thought of that," she said.

"And?"

"I think he can be trusted."

"You think he can be trusted!" her father mocked her in a tone of despair. "Well, I'm not at all sure. What does Augustus Gordon think of all this?"

"He's worried. I can always call on him by day or night. But he's getting a play into production, and he's been terribly busy lately, so I haven't seen much of him."

"He's deserted you!"

"No! He's an actor. The theater comes first with him," she said. "He'll be around to see me more often, once the play opens and he has more time."

"I should hope so. He was supposed to be your friend and Edward's friend."

"He is still my friend."

"What does he think of this?" Her father indicated the club with a sweep of his hand.

Vanessa smiled ruefully. "I'm not sure that he approves. He feels my place is on the stage. In the West

219

End with him. But that is impossible with the baby coming. This gives me an outlet and a chance to learn more about my craft. At the same time, it gets me away from Norville House.''

"Not enough. You should leave the place. I'll talk to your cold Lady Norville and tell her a thing or two," Vanessa's father stormed.

"No, Father," she said. "I have to do this my own way."

Her middle-aged actor father shook his head in despair as he said, "You always have!"

Her father remained in London for several days. She decided it would be better for him to delay presenting himself at Norville House until later. She did not entirely trust him not to lecture Lady Norville and the others on their ill-treatment of her. And she did not see that this would do any good at the moment.

He visited her at the theater studio every day, and they often had meals together. In the course of all this, he met Leonard Norville and liked him. Before leaving for rehearsals at Stratford, her father made Vanessa promise to keep in touch with him regularly and call on him if she felt herself exposed to any new threat.

"I can be here in a matter of hours," he reminded her. "If you need me, I will come."

She kissed him a warm good-bye and promised she would obey him in this. Seeing him gave her a new feeling of security. She had someone else close by on whom she could depend. Her father's long sojourn in America had come to an end, and she was grateful for this.

Now she began to audition actors and cast *Tom Jones*. She hired an excellent pianist for rehearsals and for the production itself, since there would be no place in her budget for even a small orchestra. Happily, the pianist was so capable that she felt an orchestra would not be missed in the small attic theater.

Each day, she left Norville House in the morning and did not return until evening. It was inevitable that sooner or later Lady Norville would have suspicions about what was going on. Vanessa's story that she was helping in the wig shop gave her an alibi for a while, but one evening when she returned, she found that her alibi had been demolished.

Edith Norville greeted her in the hallway and in a low voice warned her, "Be careful of your mother-in-law this evening. She's in a rage!"

"What about?" Vanessa wanted to know.

"Your secret is out," the older woman warned her. "*The Mirror* carried a story about your theater club opening today. And Lady Norville read it."

She sighed. "That really does it! I suppose they mentioned my name?"

"Several times," Edith Norville said. "They even said that Leonard had designed the sets."

"I'm sorry he was involved."

"That doesn't matter," Leonard's mother said. "There is nothing Lady Norville can say to him. He's entitled to follow his career as he likes. But she can give you a bad time, and she probably will."

"Thanks for the warning," Vanessa said. "I'll go upstairs and have a quick shower and change."

During the time she was upstairs, she decided there would be no point in denying what she'd done. The moment had come to stand up to Edward's mother. It might be unpleasant, but it was necessary.

Lady Norville was seated in her favorite chair with a

221

cocktail glass in hand when Vanessa came down to the family in the living room. The old woman glared at her.

Leonard gave Vanessa a wink of warning and went to the sideboard to fix her drink. Judge Norville stood there with an expression of embarrassment on his round crimson face, while his wife, Edith, stood by with a strained air about her.

Lady Norville spoke in an icy manner, declaring, "I have read all about your disgraceful actions in the newspaper." The cruel blue eyes of the old woman remained fixed on Vanessa as she waited for some reaction.

Vanessa stood by the easy chair in which the old woman was seated and in a light manner told her, "You mean the theater club I'm opening? There's nothing disgraceful about that."

Lady Norville said, "I think that depends on one's point of view. I consider it a low-class sort of effort in which someone bearing the title of Lady Norville should not be involved."

"I don't consider the project beneath me, if that's what you mean," Vanessa retorted.

"Further," Edward's mother snapped, "you have lied to me. Concealed what you were doing from me."

"I'm sorry about that," Vanessa said. "That was my only mistake. But you know about it now, so it's been corrected."

Lady Norville bridled at this. She told Vanessa, "You will please me by giving up this project at once. Sell your interest to someone else."

Vanessa said, "I'm afraid that's not possible."

"Of course it is!" the old woman said angrily. "Sell at a loss if you must, but remove yourself from it. And see that the Norville name is not used in any further advertisements."

Leonard brought Vanessa her drink and said, "I think Vanessa should be allowed to open her club. I'm sure the show is going to be good, and I feel it will be a money-maker."

Lady Norville shifted her anger to him. "We do not need your opinions, young man. Especially since you've also been associated with this disggaceful business."

Leonard said, "There is nothing wrong in what Vanessa is trying to do."

"It is wrong for her to become part of a public stage venture only a short time after her husband has been murdered," Lady Norville said hotly. "What do you have to say about this, anyway?"

"I'm a friend of Vanessa's," the young man said stoutly.

"No doubt!" Lady Norville jeered. "I can't forget that a scant two years ago you were living the hippie life in Soho. So who are you to judge?"

Vanessa said quickly, "There's no need for anyone to defend me. I started this on my own, and I'm not apologizing to anyone for doing it!"

Lady Norville's look of hatred matched anything she had ever offered her before. In a low voice she said, "So it's rebellion on your part. I might have expected that! We shall see!"

Nothing more was said. The subject was dropped. But Lady Norville ignored Vanessa for the balance of the evening. And Vanessa had the uneasy feeling that the old woman would use some underhanded means of getting back at her.

Leonard suggested this when he visited Vanessa at her office in the theater club the following day. The young man was obviously concerned. He said, "She'll try to cut off your funds, I'm sure."

Vanessa smiled grimly. "I'm one ahead of her on that. I'm using only money I'm entitled to. There's nothing she can do to stop me."

"I hope not."

"Don't worry about it," she said. "Right now I'm busy trying to get our second act in shape. We have an opening the first of the week, and we're not ready for it."

"I'll be back tonight," Leonard promised, rising. "I just felt I ought to warn you."

"I appreciate it," she told him. "But I think this time Lady Norville is the one who will have to give ground."

At the door of the office the young man turned to add, "I saw Augustus on the street on my way over. He's in the final stages of rehearsal with his new comedy. He opens a few nights after we do here at the club."

Vanessa said, "That's why we haven't seen or heard of him. Did he look tired?"

"Yes. He said something about my delivering a message to you about a horse. He said he'd taken delivery of it."

"I know," she said with a smile. "He's talking about Flying Anne. I made a deal to sell it to him before the rest of the stable is put up for auction."

"That was it, then," Leonard said. And he left.

Vanessa was personally directing the musical comedy. Lately she'd been rehearsing right on through the evening. The opening was set, and guests had been invited, so there could be no delaying it. The only thing to do was work harder on the rehearsals to get things in shape on time.

The dozen young people she had in the show were willing to rehearse the extra hours, and she didn't mind it. On this particular night the rehearsals went on past ten o'clock.

Around nine she was called from her chair by the piano to answer the phone in her office. It was Leonard on the line. He apologized, "I can't join you at the club tonight. We have a conference scheduled here, and I don't know when it will be over."

"That's all right," she said. "I'll get home on my own."

"It's turned foggy again," he warned her. "There's a thick yellow mist over all the city. You may have trouble getting a cab."

"There are usually more of them available here in the theater district than anywhere else," she reminded him.

"I thought of that," he agreed. "If you have any trouble, call me back here at the BBC."

"I will," she promised. "I must get back to work if we expect to finish by midnight."

As it turned out, they finished exactly twenty minutes after the midnight hour. She dismissed the cast with a cheery, "I think we have most of the big problems solved now. See you in the morning at ten."

She and the pianist exchanged a few words about an extra chorus to be sung in the second act. She said good night to the steward, who would lock up after everyone else had gone. Then she went down to search for a taxi. She had to walk to Piccadilly Circus before she was able to flag one down. And the fog was as bad as Leonard had said. She began to worry whether the fog would last for days and nights, as it sometimes did. It could spoil the club opening.

The taxi let her out in front of Norville House. The foggy night made her think of the night Edward was killed. A sudden feeling of fear took hold of her as the cab drove away and she headed for the entrance to Norville House. Nervously fumbling in her pocketbook for her keys as she neared the steps, she did not see the weird figure coming out from the shadows near the doorway to intercept her.

Chapter Twelve

When she raised her eyes she found herself staring into the ugly, gnarled face of the witch! The phantom stood crouched between her and the front door of Norville House. It was all shockingly familiar—the shawl drawn tightly around the ghost's head and the shapeless brown robe.

Vanessa screamed and staggered back as the phantom bore down on her with a knife in her upraised hand. The thick fog made a perfect setting for a murder. It would be easy to strike her down and get away, Vanessa thought frantically as she turned and ran back to the street, the phantom pursuing her.

There was no escaping, it seemed. Vanessa ran on across the cobblestone street of Blake Square, which curved between the various fine houses in a semicircle. Reaching the grass of the square, she ran on to seek refuge among the bushes. The phantom was relentless in pursuit. After screaming again, Vanessa came around the bushes and headed back across the street toward the sidewalk and entrance to Norville House, where the chase had started. She hoped by going back she would find someone wakened by her screams.

As she raced across the street with the phantom still behind her, the headlights of a car all at once appeared. The car was bringing someone to one of the houses in the square. She dodged in front of the car, which was moving slowly because of the fog. The driver pressed down on the car horn in annoyance at her antic. She paid no attention as she ran up the sidewalk and reached the door. With trembling fingers she unlocked it and let herself safely in before the phantom could reach her. The arrival of the car at that precise moment had saved her. The phantom had taken cover in the shadows.

Still sobbing quietly, she leaned against the inside of the front door. Only moments ago she had been in danger of her life. Somewhere out there in the fog the phantom was lurking. She should call the police. But what would she accomplish on such a night? They would take ages arriving, and by then her attacker would have vanished.

Norris came into the reception hall and stared at her as she stood there in the shadows. The bald man asked, "Is anything wrong, your ladyship?"

She nodded. "Yes. Someone came after me again!"

The manservant came over to her. "Just now?"

"Yes."

"Where?"

"It was that weird creature again. It appeared on the doorstep. Then it chased me across the street into the square. The only thing that saved me was a car driving in here."

"That's shocking, Lady Norville," Norris said in a worried tone. "What shall I do about it?"

Regaining some composure, she sighed and said, "That's the whole trouble. I don't believe there is anything you or anyone else can do. You can't ask the police

228

to search for a witch who died hundreds of years ago!''

"It has to be someone disguised," Norris said unhappily. "No doubt the same person who murdered Sir Edward!''

"I suspect so. But the police haven't found out much about that.''

Norris shook his head dismally. "I did not think the square would ever come to this. In the old days, there was no danger in being on the streets at night.''

"It's all quite different now," she said.

Just then Leonard appeared on the stairs. He came down to her quickly and said, "You seem to be in a state. What is it?''

She briefly told him. "I barely managed to escape this time!'' she said in conclusion.

The young man was still dressed in his street clothing. He said, "I've had enough of this! I'm going out there to take a look.''

She took him by the arm to restrain him. "No! Don't!''

He glanced down at her. "Why not? We can't let whoever it was get away without any penalty!''

"Better to do that than have you hurt," Vanessa maintained. "I saw a knife in the ghost's hand. I don't want the same thing happening to you that happened to Edward!''

Leonard's face was grim. "And I don't like to think of whoever it was getting away!'' And he broke from her grasp to rush to the door and exit.

"Please be careful!'' she cried, and went out on the step to watch him. Sick with fear, she would get a glimpse of him occasionally, and then he'd be lost in the dark and fog. At last she saw him come hurrying back, and she at once felt a deep relief.

"Nothing!'' he exclaimed with disgust.

"That's not your fault," she said.

He put an arm around her, and they went inside again. He told her, "Just the same, I must call the police. It might be of some use to them to know about the incident. This fellow was likely the same killer who finished Edward!"

"Will it do any good?"

"We have to report it," he insisted.

She sank into a chair and waited as he put the call through to the police. Suddenly she felt wearier than she ever had in her life. She'd been tired to begin with, and going through all that exertion and fright while still carrying the baby had drained her of her last ounce of fight. Again she worried that she might have done herself and the baby harm. She covered her eyes with her hand and rested.

Footsteps sounded as Leonard returned to her. His tone was tense as he said, "Do you need a doctor?"

She lifted her head and stared up at him. "I think not. But it was a dreadful experience."

"You don't feel anything unusual?"

"No," she said. "I'm just so exhausted."

"You could be dead," the young man said bitterly. "Let me help you up to your apartment." And he bent down and lifted her easily out of the chair and carried her toward the stairs.

"Thanks," she murmured, and rested her face against his shoulder as he carried her upstairs.

When they reached her apartment, he deposited her on her bed and stood by to see how she would be. He said, "Shall I rouse one of the maids to come up and help you prepare for bed?"

"I would like to have some company up here for the night," she said, gazing up wearily from her pillow. "I have seen the ghost here also. I mean, in this room!''

"You should have someone up here all the time until we get this phantom business settled," Leonard said sternly. "I'll call Norris, and he'll send up someone."

Leonard went to the phone, and she remained on the bed resting for a little. She could imagine the fuss her carping mother-in-law would create when she learned that she had asked for a maid to be installed in her apartment. But she was beyond caring.

Leonard came back to her and said, "Norris will have a maid up here shortly."

"That was thoughtful of you," she said.

"I should have thought of it before," was his reply. "The girl can sleep in the spare bedroom next to this. Then you can at least feel safe here in the apartment."

"It will make a great difference," she agreed.

"Then it's settled," Leonard said.

"What about the police?"

His young face took on an annoyed look. "They took it all down and said they would send someone here in the morning. Can you imagine that? In the morning!"

"There is a dreadful fog, and it would take them a while to get here. Then they wouldn't likely find anything more than you did."

"Just the same, they should have come at once."

"Perhaps they want to send someone familiar with the case," was her suggestion.

"No matter what you say, I can't excuse them," Leonard said with anger. "Blake Square was the scene of a murder. There could have been another murder tonight!"

"I'm sure they have some plan," she said, trying to placate the upset Leonard.

231

The situation was resolved by a sleepy-looking young maid arriving in a bathrobe and carrying her clothes in a white cotton bag. Norris accompanied her, and after introducing her to Vanessa as Nellie, he showed the girl where she would sleep.

Leonard kissed Vanessa and said, "I'll see you in the morning."

"Please do," she begged him, on her feet now. "I don't want to face those CID people with a story about a ghost all by myself!"

Thanks to the help and presence of the maid, Vanessa was able to get to bed with the minimum amount of effort and have a good night's sleep. It was fortunate that she did, for it seemed only a short time later that she was wakened by the maid with the news that someone from Scotland Yard was waiting downstairs to see her.

She sat up in bed with a groan. "First they don't come, and then they arrive at dawn."

She took a hasty shower, and again thanks to the maid, was able to dress quickly. A glance out the window told her it was still foggy. She hurried downstairs and went to the study, where she'd been directed by the maid. She found Leonard standing there talking to someone familiar to her, Inspector Halliday.

The inspector bowed slightly to her and said, "I must apologize for the early call, Lady Norville. But I'm not starting my day, I am finishing it. This visit finds me on my way home."

She said, "Thank you for coming. You must be weary. Can I order you something to drink?"

"A strong cup of black tea would be most welcome," the inspector said.

Vanessa went out and found Norris and ordered tea for

232

all of them. Then she returned to the study, where the friendly inspector was continuing to question Leonard. The Scotland Yard man at once gave his attention to her. After suggesting she be seated, he began asking her a series of questions.

"This ghost or whatever," he said, his eyes fixed on her. "Will you kindly describe it?"

She did, finishing with, "It's always the same. The same face and clothes. Like a creature from the Middle Ages."

"Fancy-dress murderer, it seems," the inspector said dryly. "They come in all varieties. Of course, there's no certainty this creature was the one who killed Sir Edward."

"I think it had to be," she said. "You know, there is a legend about the Brides of Saturn. The first Norville bride to die because she was a Capricorn was cursed by an ancient witchlike woman. The description of my attacker matches the likeness of that witch."

"Indeed?" Inspector Halliday said politely.

"But she died hundreds of years ago," Leonard complained.

"Hardly a likely suspect, then," Inspector Halliday ventured.

"Unless one believes in ghosts," Vanessa said in a bitter tone. "And I may say that more than one person in this house does believe in them."

"Interesting," Inspector Halliday said. "And perhaps helpful."

"How could a belief in ghosts be helpful to a would-be murderer?" Leonard wanted to know.

"Creates an atmosphere of fear and expectancy," Inspector Halliday explained. "Might make some singled out as victims ready to accept that a ghost would kill them. Hence weaken their struggles against any murderous attack."

"That's clever, inspector," Vanessa said.

Norris arrived with tea and scones for everyone. The inspector at once stopped his investigation to heartily attack a scone and have two cups of tea. When he'd finished, he put his notebook back in his coat pocket and prepared to depart.

He assured them, "You'll be hearing from me soon again. These things have a way of narrowing down until at last we have the solution."

They saw him to the front door, and after he'd gone, Leonard turned to her and said, "I hope his optimism is justified."

"I think he's very bright," she said.

"He'll have to be, to find out about our ghost," Leonard said grimly.

Vanessa began her day with a new feeling of confidence, despite the unpleasantness of the night before. The main reason for her bright outlook was the knowledge that from now on she would not be in the apartment alone by day or night. Having a maid there to call on made her far less afraid. She had not asked before, because she knew her mother-in-law would object. But now the chasm between herself and Lady Norville was too wide ever to be bridged. She had nothing to gain by trying to cater to the older woman.

Around noon the heavy fog lifted again. She had a full run-through of the first act of the musical before noon. And then she dismissed the company for a two-o'clock call. After this she left the attic theater to make the short journey to John Fitzgibbon's wig-and-costume shop. She wanted to see about a replacement costume for one of the principals in the *Tom Jones* presentation.

The dark old shop seemed to be empty when she first arrived, and she began to wonder if the elderly proprietor hadn't gone to lunch somewhere and in an absentminded moment left the shop unlocked. But then she heard a sound of somebody moving around upstairs, and he appeared in the shadow of the balcony, his bald head with the fringe of white hair poked over the railing.

"Yes, your ladyship," the old man said. "I was back in one of the storage rooms."

"I have a costume I'd like to get changed," she told him.

"I'll be right down," the old man said. And he made his descent of the narrow stairs quickly and crossed to her.

She showed him the costume and explained the problem. "It is suitable for the character, but it doesn't match up with the costume of the girl playing opposite him. I need something in light green rather than blue."

John Fitzgibbom took the costume in his hands and thought for a moment. "I don't think we'll have any trouble finding you something in the right color," he said. "I'll do some digging in my stock and send it over by messenger this afternoon."

"No later," she said. "I want it for the rehearsal of the second act early this evening."

"Depend on me," the old costume-shop owner said. "And if it isn't right, leave it with a note after you finish tonight. I'll get something ready in the morning. You still have your key to get in here."

She laughed. "I don't think I've ever used it."

"It could be helpful sometime," John Fitzgibbon said. "You never know."

"That's true," she said. "I must go get some lunch and return to the rehearsal."

The old man walked with her to the door. "A friend of yours was here just a little while ago."

"A friend?"

"A close friend," the old man said with a knowing smile. "Augustus Gordon!"

"Oh, Gus! How is his show coming along?"

"Having the usual problems, but Mr. Gordon is always in an upset about openings. I have no doubt it will do well. It has an Edwardian setting and costumes. I'm doing the costumes."

"So you're busy!"

"I am," the wig-and-costume man agreed. "And your other friend, Mr. Leonard Norville, has helped make me busier. He is getting a lot of his costumes for his productions with the BBC from me."

"Good!" she said.

"Augustus was asking about you," the old man said with a twinkle in his ancient eyes. "I think you'll be seeing him as soon as he gets this play on the boards."

"I hope so," she said. "I miss him. I'm very fond of him."

"And he of you," John Fitzgibbon assured her as she left.

Rehearsals went well that afternoon, and she felt that her production of *Tom Jones* was almost ready. She had learned a good deal in directing it, and now she would be able to sit back and enjoy the results of her work. If the theater club attracted enough people and turned out a financial success, there would be other plays later. In the meantime, she could go through her pregnancy with the heavy work of getting the club under way completed.

On Sunday afternoon she had the final run-through of the show. Leonard was too busy with a new series at the BBC to attend, but he had promised to be on hand opening night. She'd also sent invitations to a number of other people, including Augustus Gordon.

The star phoned her and said, "I'll try to make it late in the evening, Vanessa. I want to be there, but I'm having my own opening night on Wednesday."

"I understand," she told him. "And I won't be angry if you don't make it."

Augustus Gordon said, "I'll manage somehow, and I have house tickets for you and Leonard for my opening."

Because she knew opening night would be a strain, Vanessa decided to go to bed early on Sunday night and get all the rest she could. She felt less afraid of the old mansion and had fewer bad dreams now that she had a maid in the apartment. But the terrifying memory of the witch still haunted her at times. The ugly, lined face and the crouched figure remained a forbidding specter in the back of her mind.

Rain had begun early Sunday afternoon, and by evening the downpour was torrential. She was about to prepare for bed when the phone rang.

She answered it and at first didn't recognize the voice at the other end of the line. Then she realized it was Leonard, but he sounded strangely different. She said, "I hardly knew who you were."

Leonard said, "I have a bad connection here. I'm calling because I must see you."

"Tonight?" she asked, in surprise.

"Yes," he said. "I've gained some interesting information. I think I can tell you who killed Edward!"

She gasped. "Tell me!"

"Not on the phone," he said. "Better we meet somewhere. I don't want to discuss it at the house, either."

"Where do you want me to meet you?"

He said, "At John Fitzgibbon's shop. You have a key, and so do I. It's the ideal spot."

"Why not my theater club?"

"Aren't the stage crew working there tonight?"

"I'd forgotten," she admitted. "There could be someone there. But I'm not certain. I could call."

"No, it's easier to meet at the wig shop. I can be there in thirty minutes," Leonard said. "What about you?"

"I'll leave at once," she said. "With luck, I'll get a taxi."

"Fine," Leonard said. "I wouldn't suggest this, but it is something we can't put off."

"I agree," she said.

As soon as she put down the phone, she found her raincoat, plastic kerchief, and umbrella. Then she quickly made her way downstairs.

Norris was in the hallway and showed surprise when he saw her descending the stairs. He asked, "Are you going out, your ladyship?"

"Yes, I have to," she said. "I'm meeting Mr. Leonard at the wig shop. He has some important information for me."

"Let me get you a cab," Norris said.

"Do you think you can?"

"It shouldn't be too difficult," Norris said. And he put on his raincape and took an umbrella from the stand and went out into the cold downpour to try to hail a taxi.

He was gone no more than five minutes when he returned with a taxi and helped her into it. She gave the driver the address of the wig shop and sat back with closed eyes as the cab began the journey through the dark, wet streets.

She asked herself what information Leonard might have come upon. And who had offered it to him. Her tension grew as she thought about it, and she became convinced that someone within Norville House must bear the guilt of the attacks on her. Perhaps it had been a plot between Lady Madeline Smith and someone else who had something to gain. But who?

By the time the cab halted outside the wig shop, Vanessa was in a nervous, taut state. She paid the driver and rushed to the door of the shop. It was still raining hard, and the door was locked. She found her key and opened it and stepped into its familiar musty atmosphere. The shop was in almost complete darkness, with only a small night-light on the wall at the back providing a limited glow of murky yellow light.

She stood near the door waiting. Then, becoming restless, she strolled to the rear of the shop under the balcony. It was here that the single night-line shone. She was uneasy at being alone in the old shop, and standing within the glow of the light made her less afraid.

It had to be thirty minutes since she'd received the phone call, and still Leonard hadn't arrived. She noted that it was raining even harder than before and decided the storm might be responsible for his being so late in meeting her.

Suddenly she saw the dark outline of a man at the door of the shop, and a moment later he entered. She rushed the length of the shop to meet Leonard, but when she came up to him, she was startled to see that it was someone else.

"Gus!" she exclaimed. "What are you doing here?"

The handsome actor removed his raincoat and folded it

over his arm. "Leonard called and asked me to come here for a meeting with you two. Something to do with Edward's killer."

She nodded. "He insisted I come for the same reason, but he didn't mention that you would be here."

"Probably because I told him I wasn't sure I could make it," the star complained. "I left a rehearsal to join you."

"Thank you, Gus," she said with gratitude. "Leonard ought to be here any minute now. He's late."

"I hope so," Augustus Gordon said, gazing down the length of the dark store at the door. "I have to return to my rehearsal."

"How is it going?"

"Rocky," the star said moodily. "I've had to change a number of costumes at the last minute. Fitzgibbon is working on them upstairs."

"Oh?"

He suggested, "I'll take you up, and we'll see how he's doing. The materials ought to be all laid out on his work-bench. It will fill in the time."

"All right," she said. The idea appealed to her, since she was becoming steadily more edgy waiting for Leonard.

Augustus led the way up the stairs to the balcony and then took her through a door to the big storage and work room beyond. He switched on the lights to reveal racks of costumes stored along the walls and several worktables.

The worktables were in the middle of the big room, and the star went over and examined a costume in the making on one of them. He said, "Come over and look at this! It will give you an idea of our problem."

She crossed to the table and studied the half-completed

costume. She was about to ask him about it, but she never did get around to it. As she stood there, she was suddenly seized by the arms and forcibly dragged across to a wooden armchair.

As the star thrust her down into the chair she cried out, "What's the matter? Have you lost your mind?" And she struggled to free herself.

It was a hopeless struggle. Augustus Gordon had cloth strips by the chair, and he was now expertly tying her in the chair with them. In a few minutes she was a helpless captive, with her arms and legs bound tightly to the chair.

The situation was so mad, and it had happened so suddenly, she was left stunned. She stared up at the handsome star and demanded, "What kind of madness is this?"

"No madness," the handsome star said in his mocking way. "It's time you and I had a serious talk!"

"You didn't need to truss me up like this to talk," she exclaimed indignantly. "Wait until Leonard gets here!"

He smiled. "Leonard isn't coming!"

"He is! He called me on the phone!"

"I called you on the phone," Augustus Gordon said smugly. "Not a bad imitation, either, though you did worry me by saying I didn't sound quite like Leonard!"

"You?" she gasped.

He nodded. "Yes. So now you know there is no one coming to disturb us."

"Why?" she asked, panic in her voice. "Why are you doing this?"

"Because you have behaved so stupidly," the star said. "It began with your deciding to give up the stage and marry Edward. You chose him when you could have had me as a husband!"

241

"I loved Edward," she said.

"I'm not sure love is an emotion that you were able to afford," the tall, handsome man said with that mocking smile still on his face. An insane smile, it seemed to her now. "You became Lady Norville too easily!"

"You were supposed to be our friend!"

"I gave you that impression," he said suavely. "But I was never Edward's friend. And when you married him, you also became my enemy, especially when you became pregnant with his child."

"Why?" she asked in terror.

"Because you stood in my way," the actor told her. "You see, long before I introduced you to Edward, I had made up my mind he would die."

"Edward trusted you! How could you plot against his life?"

"Because he was living the life that was rightfully mine," the star replied. "I knew about the secret passages that led to Norville House. I learned to use them and adopted the disguise of the wicked witch! Almost a Disney touch!"

"You were the one!" she said accusingly.

"I killed Edward and came into the house to attack you. I almost succeeded in finishing you and making it seem an accident. Then you had that maid come into the apartment, so I have had to change the scene of my operations to here. You will die here!"

"What reason have you for killing me?" she sobbed.

"The best of all reasons," Augustus Gordon said. "You are standing in the way of my claim to the Norville title. The sealed envelope your lawyer has contains instructions in the event Edward died without wife or heir. I found a way into his office one night, read the contents,

242

and then resealed the envelope. With you out of the way, that will be settled. And the will names me as Edward's illegitimate half-brother and next in succession. My father did that little for me before he died. He thought I would never benefit by his gesture, and in the end, I, like my mother, would be given nothing. But I've changed the plot, you see!''

Vanessa stared up at his mocking face with horror. She said tautly, ''You told me from the first you had always wanted to live Edward's life. But I didn't understand.''

''Now you do!''

''It won't work!'' she told him. ''You'll have to pay for murdering me!''

''I don't intend to murder you, Vanessa, darling,'' he said smoothly. ''You are going to die in an accident. You came down here in answer to a hoax call to meet Leonard. He didn't appear, but in the meanwhile, a fire suddenly broke out in the shop. The wiring is old and faulty, and you were trapped in the smoke and flames. The flames will take care of the cloth ties holding you to the chair, so there need be no suspicions. I had an expert devise the means to start the fire so it won't be discovered.''

''You wouldn't dare go through with it!'' she cried in despair, knowing that the statement was senseless.

He offered her that mocking smile again. ''I certainly can't back away now that I've told you all this.'' And with that he calmly went over and snapped off the lights. He told her, ''The device is attached to the lines of this light switch. Within a few minutes the fire will begin.''

And she heard his footsteps trail off as she sat there in the darkness. She tried to tell herself that it was all a nightmare. That she was back in her bed in Norville House having a bad dream. None of this could really happen. But the cloth ties were cutting off the circulation in her hands and feet, making them numb. She struggled in a hopeless attempt to escape, and then bowed her head and began a steady sobbing.

Maybe five minutes passed before she first smelled the smoke. Her terror became overwhelming as the smoke increased, and now she could hear a crackling in the walls and feel the heat. She began to choke on the smoke, and her eyes streamed with tears from its acrid bite. As she coughed and struggled for breath, she felt some small comfort in the knowledge that she would become unconscious and die from suffocation before the flames reached her.

The minutes were now centuries long and filled with frightening nightmares and tortures! She was gasping for breath when she saw the figure come groping over to her. She sobbed, "Help me! Help me!"

"Vanessa!" And this time it was Leonard's voice and not someone imitating him.

She somehow conveyed what had happened in a few gasped words as he untied her from the chair. She was too weak to stand on her feet, and so he carried her out of the shop and into the rain-ridden street for safety. He put her down in a doorway and then rushed off to the nearest fire-alarm box.

Vanessa hunched in the wet doorway, still coughing and fighting for her breath, her eyes stinging from the smoke. Across the street was the wigmaker's shop, and now she could see the tongues of flame devouring it.

A breathless Leonard returned to her. "Did he not come back here to you?"

She glanced up, fear in her eyes. "No!"

"I saw him when I was at the fire-alarm box," Leonard

said. "He dodged into this street and vanished. I came racing back as soon as I gave the alarm. I was sure he'd try to attack you again!"

"I didn't see him," she said.

Leonard knelt by her in the rain-swept doorway. "He knows he's failed, and he'll try to get away!"

"Where can he go?"

"I don't know!"

She asked, "How did you know where I was?"

He gave her a troubled look. "Norris told me. He said you had come here to meet me. I knew something was wrong, so I followed."

Their talk was interrupted by the clamor of the fire engines arriving. The fire fighters at once went to work in an attempt to save the wigmaker's shop, but it was too late. The ancient building was gutted by flames, though the buildings on either side were saved.

Augustus Gordon did not travel farther than his smart West End apartment. He was found there in the bedroom the following morning with a bullet wound in his temple. Vanessa told her story to Inspector Halliday. The inspector visited the Norville family solicitor, and the sealed letter was opened and confirmed it all. Then the letter was destroyed.

Vanessa recovered from her shattering experience and continued to live at Norville House. One result of her near-brush with death was a change of attitude on the part of her cold mother-in-law. Lady Norville was finally almost kindly toward her.

Five months later a daughter was born to Vanessa and the late Sir Edward in a hospital not far from Norville House. So it was not surprising that her first visitors were the various members of her husband's family.

Judge James Norville and the matronly Edith were the first to visit Vanessa and the baby. The old judge chuckled and declared, "She's a Norville! You can tell! I honestly think she resembles me."

Vanessa smiled and glanced at the child beside her. "At least she has your round red face!"

Edith tugged at her husband's arm. "There are others to see Vanessa. Don't stand there pretending to be the proud grandfather. You're merely the child's great-uncle."

"Good enough!" the judge said happily. "We'll be by soon again, Vanessa."

"Thank you," she said. "I hope to return to Norville House within a few days."

The two left the room, and then the door opened hesitantly and a chastened Lady Norville came slowly into the room and over to the bedside.

The older woman gazed down at Vanessa and the baby and in an emotion-choked voice told her, "It's a lovely child! Like Edward being born again. And I've been so unfair to you!"

"That's forgotten," Vanessa said. "This is a fresh beginning for all of us."

Lady Norville's eyes filled with tears, and with a silent nod she turned and left the room.

The final visitor was the most important, as far as Vanessa was concerned. Leonard came in smiling and kissed her and then touched the baby's cheek affectionately with a forefinger. "I called your father," he said. "He's coming here tomorrow. Says he's delighted to have another actress in the family."

Vanessa laughed. "That sounds like him! After all the struggle I had to get on the stage!"

"You made it!" Leonard said, studying her with affection. "Your theater club is a big success. And thanks to you I have my own career! You gave me some of your Capricorn courage!"

Vanessa glanced at the baby with loving eyes. "It may be more difficult for her. She's not a Capricorn."

"You will make up for that," Leonard said. "I'm not at all worried about her future. Or the future of any of us now that the legend has been shattered."

She raised her eyes to him. "The curse of the Brides of Saturn! Augustus became part of it! Perhaps he couldn't really help himself! The fates assigned him his role."

"However it was, it is over," Leonard told her. "The curse doesn't apply to me since I'm not the heir. I can take myself a Capricorn bride whenever I find one willing.'

Vanessa smiled and lifted her hand for him to take.

BERKLEY'S SUSPENSE FILLED GOTHIC SERIES FEATURES A BOOK FOR EACH SIGN OF THE ZODIAC